DOCTOR WHO – TERMINUS

DOCTOR WHO
TERMINUS

Based on the BBC television serial by Steve Gallagher by
arrangement with the British Broadcasting Corporation

JOHN LYDECKER

A TARGET BOOK
published by
The Paperback Division of
W. H. ALLEN & Co. Ltd

A Target Book
Published in 1983
By the Paperback Division of W.H. Allen & Co. Ltd
A Howard & Wyndham Company
44 Hill Street, London W1X 8LB

First published in Great Britain by
W.H. Allen & Co. Ltd 1983

Phototypeset by Sunrise Setting, Torquay, Devon
Printed and bound in Great Britain by
Hunt Barnard Printing Ltd, Aylesbury, Bucks.

ISBN 0 426 19385 7

Tegan was sure that there must be something to like about Turlough, but she couldn't think what. It wasn't his age, it wasn't his looks – it wasn't anything that she could name, but as they walked down the TARDIS corridor his presence behind her gave Tegan a creepy feeling between the shoulders. It was like stories she'd heard of travellers back home in the Australian bush; they'd get the same crawling sensation and look down to see a snake about to strike.

'These are all storerooms,' she said, gesturing at a set of doors she was certain she'd never seen before, and she carried on past before Turlough could ask any awkward questions. *Just give him the tour, Tegan,* the Doctor had said, *you know your way around by now,* and she was left in the position of either tackling the job or else arguing for her own incompetence – which she wasn't going to do, not in front of the Brat. Her assessment of Turlough was such that she'd trust him to store up the admission and use it to embarrass her sometime. It was about the *only* thing she'd trust him for.

At the next intersection, she stopped and glanced back. Turlough was looking the doors over as if he was weighing up whether or not to believe her. In the cool grey light of the timeless corridors he looked serene, almost angelic, but when he caught her eye and smiled there was a glint of something hard and unpleasant under the surface. If the Doctor looked for long enough, he'd probably see it as well... but then he'd never had reason to, and on the couple of occasions when she and Nyssa had tried to describe their doubts he'd dismissed them. Reservations about a new companion in the TARDIS could so easily look like a display of petty jealousy; and when the Doctor was around, Turlough's act was very, very good.

He sauntered along slowly to catch up, and Tegan turned the corner. She saw with relief that, at last, they were coming into an area she recognised. Not only was so much of the TARDIS unfamiliar, she was convinced that parts of the craft quietly redesigned themselves when no one was looking.

Through this open area and out the other side, and they'd come to the corridor with the main living areas. She slowed, so that Turlough could make up the distance. He didn't hurry. Something else that had unsettled her; Turlough was no primitive, but there had been nothing in his background to prepare him for the intellectual and sensual shock of entering a craft containing the floorplan of a mansion in an external package the size of an old-earth police telephone box. So why was he taking it all so calmly?

'Well,' she said as they reached the living space, 'that's the layout.' She tried not to sound too relieved at making it back.

'It goes on forever,' Turlough said politely, as if he was thanking an aunt for a present (*but he ought to be standing there with his mouth hanging open and his mind completely blown*, Tegan thought).

'It can seem like it,' she said. 'It's best if you don't go wandering until you know your way around.'

'How am I supposed to manage?'

'Give me a call.' *That's a joke*, she thought, and pointed across the corridor to the door of the room that she shared with Nyssa. 'Most of the time I'll be over there.'

'Don't I get a room?'

'I was coming to that next.'

Well, to be honest, she'd been putting it off for as long as she could. She led him down to another of the doors and touched for it to open. 'This one... isn't being used,' she said delicately.

Turlough went through and stood in the middle of the room, looking around. Tegan hesitated for a moment before she followed. This was Adric's old room. Nothing inside had been touched or moved since they'd lost him. She could understand that it was only fair to let Turlough have somewhere that was within easy distance of the console room and the social areas, but why did it have to be *here*?

She knew the answer, of course; that the pain was a necessary part of the healing. But it didn't make her feel any better.

'It looks like a kid's room,' Turlough said.

Tegan did her best to keep the anger out of her voice. She almost succeeded. 'It was Adric's.'

'Who?'

'It doesn't matter. But he wasn't a child.'

Turlough barely seemed to have noticed. 'I've had enough of children,' he said, 'what with that awful school on Earth.'

She relented a little. 'Maybe the Doctor was right, and she simply wasn't giving him a chance. She said,

'You can change things around to suit yourself.'

He picked up an interlocking mathematical puzzle from the desk, inspected it, and tossed it back. It rolled and landed on a heap of notes and charts. 'All this can go, for a start,' he said, and then he looked up and smiled. Practising for the Doctor. 'That's not unreasonable, is it?'

'Do what you like,' Tegan said stiffly. 'It's your place.' And she turned and walked out.

When she was back in the corridor, she had to stop and take a deep breath. Steady, now, girl, don't let him get to you. That's how he works – he'll needle away until you explode, and then he'll stand there in complete innocence while you make a fool of yourself. But why? We've taken him in, sheltered him... why isn't it enough?

She stood under the corridor lights and listened to the even heartbeat of the TARDIS all around her. It was a good trick for getting calm. Tegan got half-way there, deciding it was the best she was going to manage, and went through to join Nyssa in their shared room.

'He's got the manners of a pig,' she said.

Nyssa looked up from her work, surprised. 'The Doctor?'

'The brat! I had to show him all around the TARDIS. You'd think he was going to buy it.'

'Perhaps he'll settle down,' Nyssa suggested, but Tegan wasn't about to be reassured.

'You know he threatened me?' she said.

Nyssa laid aside the abacus that she'd been using to check over some data. 'Seriously?'

'It seemed serious enough at the time.'

'Why?'

'I found him playing around with a roundel. He tried to laugh it off, but he's up to something.'

'Have you told the Doctor?'

'Not yet.' And perhaps not ever, if Turlough managed to keep the Doctor convinced with his pretence of innocence.

Nyssa pushed herself back from the bench. Most of its surface was taken up with the intricate glassware tangle of a biochemical experiment, like a funfair modelled in miniature. She said, 'Well, that means two of us are having a less than perfect day.'

'Not you, as well,' Tegan said, and she came over to take a look at the set-up on the bench. Nyssa had been saying for some time now that she felt she was losing her grip on all that she'd learned, and that it was time she went over some of the basics of the disciplines she'd acquired on her lost home world of Traken. The glassware and the spectral analyser had all come from the TARDIS's extensive but haphazardly organised stores, maybe even from one of the rooms that Tegan had identified to Turlough in passing. There wasn't much here that she could recognise, except for the shallow glass dishes in which bacterial cultures were growing and, of course, the book that Nyssa was using for reference. Of all the storage and information retrieval technologies available to the TARDIS, the Doctor insisted that books were the best. To put all of your faith in any more sophisticated system, he would say, is to ask for trouble; when a crisis hits and the lights go out, the time you need your information most is the very time that you can't get to it. He called it a *Catch-22* situation. And when Nyssa wanted to know what a *Catch-22* situation was, the Doctor sent her to the TARDIS's library – Earth, Literature

(North American), twentieth century (third quarter).

Tegan said, 'What's the experiment?'

'I'm trying to synthesise an enzyme. It's one of the simpler procedures on the course, but it isn't going right. I'm way out of practice.'

'I thought you did this last time you had one of these blitzes. It went okay then.'

Nyssa sighed. 'I know, but then I had Adric to do the calculation for me. This time I'm using my own figures, and they're nowhere near as good. I've got a lot more ground to cover before I can afford to get lazy again.' She looked despondently at the equipment and at the pages of notes that she'd scattered over every unoccupied space on the bench. This was to have been her occupation at one time; now it seemed that it was her last link with Traken, and she was in danger of losing it.

Tegan said, 'Why don't I dig out Adric's notes for you?'

'I really ought to do it myself.'

'Come on, cheat a little. My old teacher always said if you don't know, ask.'

'That sounds fair enough.'

'I know, but then she'd whack us for not paying attention in the first place. What do you say?'

Nyssa shook her head. 'I wouldn't know where to look.'

But Tegan was already on her way to the door. 'Adric kept files, didn't he?' she said. 'Besides, it gives me a chance to check up on you-know-who.'

Tegan was on her way to a surprise. Turlough was not, as she was expecting, making a big heap of Adric's possessions in the middle of the floor of his new room;

he wasn't even in his new room. As soon as Tegan had left him, he'd switched off his smile like a lightbulb and followed her to the door; he'd watched as she stood out in the corridor and struggled for self-control, and when she'd disappeared into her own room he slipped out and tiptoed past. He was tense, ready to alter his manner in a moment; the Doctor was out here, somewhere. If they met, Turlough had a plausible story ready. He wasn't quite sure what it might be, but extemporisation to suit the moment was his main talent. It was why he'd been chosen.

He'd annoyed Tegan. Well, so what – Tegan wasn't the one who mattered. As far as the Doctor was concerned, Turlough's act so far had been flawless. Anything the two girls might say would look like jealous sniping; it would help his case and weaken theirs. He couldn't lose.

In spite of the uncertain nature of the tour that he'd been given, he'd fixed the main points of the TARDIS layout in his mind. It was much as he'd been led to expect. He got to the console room without meeting the Doctor, and outside the door he stopped and listened for a few seconds. He heard nothing other than the regular motion of the time rotor, and after a moment he strolled in. *Turlough, wide-eyed and innocent, come to see if he can be of any use around the place* … He let the attitude drop as soon as he was sure that he was alone.

With the exception of an old beechwood coat-stand that the Doctor had found useful in one of his more flamboyant incarnations, the console room was empty of furniture. Not that it would have been difficult to single out the TARDIS's main control desk; the angular structure with its central rotor dominated the

11

chamber, the translucent core rising and falling as if in time with the very breathing of the craft. Turlough circled it, slowly. The technology was alien to him, the layout of the controls unfamiliar. A wrong move now could ruin all that he'd achieved. He'd come so far on his own. Now it was time to get help.

He reached deep into his pocket and brought out a tiny cube. It looked harmless enough. If he'd been searched he could have claimed that it was some kind of memento or souvenir, a worthless crystal mined by a great-uncle and passed down through the family for its sentimental value. Turlough didn't know whether he had any great-uncles or not; if he did, the chances were that none of them had been engaged in anything quite so honest and hardworking as the mining trade. The point was that the story sounded plausible. He set the cube on a flat surface of the console, and then he crouched to stare into it.

The crystal structure of the cube had been altered to key in with Turlough's mindwave. Only he could unlock it. After a few moments' concentration, the cube began to glow; Turlough waited for it to reach peak brightness before he spoke.

'I did as you said. They've accepted me.' He kept his voice low, knowing that it would still be possible to lose the game even now that he was within reach – literally – of its end. There was a pause before the voice of his unseen controller, harsh and distorted, came through.

'*Acceptance is not enough. You must destroy.*'

'I'm in the console room. Tell me what I have to do.'

A series of terse instructions followed. As Turlough was following them through, lifting one of the access panels beneath the console and identifying some of the major components beneath to give himself some orientation, Tegan was crossing the corridor some distance away on an errand that she would never complete.

The interior of the console was unbelievably complicated; without step-by-step guidance, Turlough wouldn't have had a chance. He rested his finger-tips against the sides of the single element that the search had led him to. It felt slightly loose in its mount; a decent grip and a good pull would probably get it free completely.

'What will this do?.' he whispered.

'You are touching the heart of the TARDIS. Rip it free!'

But Turlough immediately withdrew his hand a little. 'And what happens to me?'

'You will be saved. I am ready to lift you away. You'll live forever at my side.'

Being saved and living forever sounded attractive enough, but Turlough wasn't so sure about the prospect of eternity spent at the side of the owner of the unseen voice. It was probably just the Black Guardian's way of saying he'd be grateful. Turlough certainly hoped so. He suppressed a little shiver, and re-established his grip on the component deep inside the console. He pulled.

The console reacted immediately. The time rotor locked in place and started to flicker, the lights in the console room dimmed momentarily, and alarm buzzers on the control panels started to make urgent noises. The component came half-way out, and then jammed.

Turlough pulled harder, but he couldn't get it free.

13

Half a job would accomplish nothing; worse, it would ruin his cover with the Doctor and destroy the Black Guardian's confidence in him. Desperately he tried again; he lost his grip and some of the skin from a knuckle as his hand slipped free.

'It's stuck,' he told the contact cube. 'It won't move any more.' Turlough's mind was racing; if he couldn't succeed, how could he patch up the situation and give himself a second chance? *Come on*, he told himself, *think on your feet, it's what you're good at*, but just when he needed his talent most, it seemed to have taken a walk. He pushed the component back into place as best he could. It didn't feel right – he'd probably broken connections that would have to be re-made by someone who knew what they were doing, but for now he would have to be satisfied with making everything look normal. He withdrew his hand and started to replace the cover panels.

The Black Guardian didn't like it. '*Continue!*' The cube pulsed. '*Continue!*'

'I can't. There isn't time.'

'*The breakup is beginning. You must...*'

Turlough snatched the cube from the console surface and pocketed it. His controller was silenced, the glow which signified contact dying as soon as he picked it up. He raised himself from his knees and looked around; the rotor was still locked and the alarms were still sounding. He could run from the console room, but if the others were approaching it would be a big mistake; no amount of explanation could remove the appearance of guilt even from the Doctor's mind. He could claim some innocent act of incompetence, perhaps knocking a control without meaning to, but that could be easily checked. At best,

14

he'd be barred from the console room and closely watched whenever he came near to any area of importance; there would be no second chances that way.

He'd have to stay where he was. He'd heard the alarms and had come running to see if he could help. That ought to do it.

With an eye on the door, Turlough started to work on the expression he'd be using when they caught up with him.

Some problems, the Doctor believed, were best solved through quiet reflection. Many of the decisions that he'd had to make in the recent past had been made under pressure – and they hadn't, he had to admit, all been for the best. He was, he thought, a social animal – more so than any other Time Lord that he'd known, although he'd always regarded himself as something of a rebel – but there were times when he needed to be alone. It was a basic requirement, human or otherwise, and it was in recognition of this that he'd asked Tegan to install the newcomer in Adric's old room. But as far as the Doctor was concerned, staying in one place for too long made him restless; when there was a problem to be tackled, like the resolution of the spiky relationship between the two girls and Turlough, he preferred to be out and roaming.

There was also another advantage. It meant that you couldn't easily be found and distracted.

But as the Doctor emerged on his wandering from the half-lit tunnels where the inhibitor crystals were stacked in their pressurised tanks, the urgent, half-panicky note in Tegan's calling told him that there was more serious business to be attended to. His name echoed faintly through the corridor complex, and he started out towards its source.

Something was badly wrong. Tegan had always been wary in strange situations, but she was no coward; and as the Doctor reached her and she spun around to meet him, it was obvious that she was scared.

'All right, Tegan,' the Doctor said, aiming to calm her down in order to get as much information as he could, 'what's the problem?'

But Tegan could only shake her head. She was breathless from running. 'You'd better come,' was all she could say, and so the Doctor nodded and followed as she led the way.

Crisis had improved Tegan's navigational ability considerably. She made straight for the residential corridor leading to the console room, and as they rounded the final corner it became obvious to the Doctor why he was needed. He stopped for a moment, and then walked forward slowly.

He'd never seen anything like it, not on the inside of the TARDIS. One complete wall of the corridor was starting to break away. The effect was difficult to appreciate. The wall seemed to shimmer from floor to ceiling, as if it wasn't a solid surface at all but a cut-out piece of a waterfall; it sparkled with drowned stars and pulsed like the heartbeat of a sick machine. The Doctor was tempted to touch it, but he knew better.

'What is it?' Tegan said.

The Doctor was still watching, trying to make out whether the breakup was stable or getting any worse. It seemed to be deteriorating. 'It's the matrix,' he told her. 'We're in trouble.'

'And Nyssa's on the other side!'

The Doctor stared at her for a moment, and then he turned and headed for the console room at speed. Tegan followed, only a couple of paces behind.

Turlough was already there when they entered. He seemed lost and confused by the console alarms, and his relief when the Doctor arrived was obvious.

The first thing the Doctor did was to look over the telltales on the console. There was no clue to the cause of the problem to be found there, but the rotor was still jammed and flickering. 'What was Nyssa working on?' he asked.

Tegan was still by his side. 'Nothing that would cause this,' she said emphatically.

The Doctor didn't press it further. Tegan didn't have a hard-science background, but her grasp of the uses and consequences of technology was good. Besides, Nyssa wasn't likely to be dabbling in anything that would have this kind of effect. She hadn't told him what she was proposing to do – mostly because she was afraid of being given helpful advice when she really thought she should manage alone – but her field was the biological sciences, not high-energy physics.

And now she was trapped in a section of the TARDIS that was tearing itself apart.

The Doctor started lifting panels to get to the circuitry inside. The breakup that he'd witnessed was something that simply shouldn't happen, but it was useless to insist on the point. Safety cut-outs were an integral part of the console; whatever happened to the TARDIS, it was designed to keep its internal structure solid right up to the end.

But tell that to the TARDIS. He started to trace the

lines in and out of the matrix generator, looking for anything that could give him a clue about the cause of the trouble. As long as Nyssa hadn't actually been in contact with the inside wall when the trouble started, she was probably still all right; but unless he could arrest and reverse the instability, it would creep forward and surround her and then, finally, absorb her. And then the rest of the TARDIS would start to follow.

There seemed to be nothing wrong, nothing at all. Every line was intact and there were none of the telltale signs of failure that would *have* to be there before such a deterioration could take place. His hand came to rest on the main cut-out stack; the stack came free.

He realised with horror that he was able to pull the component nearly all of the way out; the TARDIS was holding together almost entirely on its subsidiaries. The Doctor looked up sharply. He said, 'Has anybody been lifting these panels?'

Turlough looked immediately at Tegan. 'Not that I know of,' he said. Tegan started to blush, even though there was no reason why she should. She couldn't help it.

'The cut-out's been disturbed. The stabilising control on the space-time element. It's what holds the TARDIS together.'

Turlough came in for a closer look, and the Doctor had him hold one of the contacts closed as he worked. Tegan watched for a minute, but she couldn't stay silent; 'What about Nyssa?' she said.

The Doctor reached across the console to operate the switch that would uncover the large screen on the console room wall. 'I'm trying to re-focus the exterior

18

viewer on the inside of the TARDIS,' he said, and as he spoke something crackled inside the console and threw out a rain of sparks. It made him hesitate, but only for a moment. 'Watch the screen,' he said, 'and tell me what you see.'

The screen cover rolled back, and the Doctor's attention returned to the depths of the console. Tegan watched as the screen came alive, but there was no recognisable picture. 'Just a mess,' she reported.

The Doctor glanced up. 'Dimensional instability,' he said, shaking his head. There was no way that he could do a fast repair on the cut-out. It was a lengthy and intricate job, and the danger to Nyssa – already considerable – was increasing minute by minute.

He managed to get the viewer focused on the interior of the room. It was something he'd never tried before. In theory it ought to work... but then he'd had a theory about the stability of the matrix, as well. He opened the channel that would carry two-way sound, and said, 'Nyssa? Nyssa, can you hear me?'

'We're getting a picture!' Tegan said excitedly. Turlough had moved back and was watching from beside her.

The image was torn about by interference, but at least it was recognisable. Nyssa had backed up against the table that carried her experimental gear. The textbook that she'd been using was clutched tightly under her arm. Although she was obviously scared, she was still in control; even as the Doctor's voice broke through, she was clearly looking around for some means of diverting the danger.

This had been the Doctor's main worry, the reason why he had made a priority out of establishing communication with Nyssa. If she'd assumed that the

19

distortion around her was the result of some inpouring of energy, she might attempt to channel it away from herself. But the lightning-rod theory wouldn't just be ineffective, it would be fatal; in a burning house, one doesn't feed the flames.

'I hear you!' she said. Her relief was twofold; until now she'd had no way of knowing whether the rest of the TARDIS and its occupants were still whole.

'Stay well back, Nyssa,' the Doctor warned, 'there's nothing you can do.'

The screen image broke up for a moment. When it reformed, Nyssa was backing around the table. 'Can't I conduct it away?' she was saying.

'No. I'm trying to contain it from this end.' He wouldn't have much time. Already the breakup was starting to show, creeping in from the edge of the screen.

They lost the image again. Turlough watched over the Doctor's shoulder as he worked to restore it, with the result that only Tegan saw what happened next. The picture returned but she was convinced that, for a moment, it was the wrong picture; it showed a curving interior wall that was the wrong shape and the wrong colour, and there was something *else*... something that sent her heart racing as if it had been spiked, something that faded before she'd even had the chance to be sure of what it was. The more familiar image came through, but it showed even more interference than before.

'Something's happening in there,' she said.

The Doctor looked up. 'What?'

'I don't know. For a moment it didn't look like a part of the TARDIS.'

The Doctor took a deep breath. 'The outside

20

universe is breaking through. I'm losing it.'

'What are you going to do?'

When she'd asked the question, Tegan waited. The Doctor didn't reply immediately, and Tegan felt a growing horror; for all the occasional vagueness of his moods and his unpredictable behaviour, he was never indecisive. Hesitation now could only mean one thing. The Doctor was out of options.

This was closer to the truth than the Doctor would have cared to admit. The TARDIS was like a bubble of space and time, the job of the matrix being to maintain the bubble. The deterioration of the residential corridor was only the beginning of what would ultimately be a complete collapse.

Orthodox methods of operation simply didn't allow for this kind of situation. There was nothing he could do to save Nyssa, and within a short time the rest of them could expect to share her fate.

As long as he stuck to orthodox methods.

'I'm going to make an emergency exit,' he said with renewed determination, and he opened another panel along from the matrix circuitry.

As the Doctor worked on, Tegan watched the screen. Nyssa had gone about as far back as she could get, and now the creeping instability was starting to engulf her bench experiment; the glassware exploded and forced her to cover her face as the shimmering moved in, a net that was slowly drawing closed around her. Tegan screwed her fists tight in frustration; there wasn't a thing she could do to help, and it was burning her up. Turlough watched alongside her. His eyes didn't move from the Doctor; perhaps his anxiety was all reserved for his own future.

The Doctor popped up from behind the console.

'Nyssa,' he said, 'look behind you!'

Tegan saw Nyssa turn, and she wondered what the Doctor meant. And then she saw; something was happening to the back wall of the room. The normal grey-and-white interior moulding of the TARDIS was starting to fade away and to be replaced by a new texture. Nyssa stood before a large door. It was metal and monstrously solid, as if it had been built to withstand tons of pressure, but the garbled representation of the room's interior could show them no more detail than this. The door was starting to swing open on its own. Nyssa took a step back, and almost retreated into the field of instability.

'Go through!' the Doctor called to her. 'It's your only chance!'

'But where are you sending her?' Tegan said, bewildered.

'I don't know,' the Doctor admitted. 'But if she stays, she'll...' Whatever he was going to say, it was drowned by a roar of static. The screen turned unbearably white, a window on Armageddon. Dimensional instability had finally consumed the entire section of the TARDIS; now they could only wait and hope that it would die out rather than spread.

They could also hope that Nyssa had moved quickly enough.

The screen cleared slowly – too slowly, it seemed at first, but as the image re-formed they could make out the fact that the room had just about managed to hold its shape. The shimmering was spasmodic, much less violent than before although no less deadly. There was no sign of Nyssa at all.

The unfamiliar door that was the TARDIS's temporary gateway to the outside stood open.

Beyond it was darkness, and the contrast range of the screen couldn't handle the shadow detail. Turlough said that he thought he'd seen something move, and it occurred to the Doctor that Nyssa might be trying to re-enter the room, 'Keep moving!' he shouted to her, 'It isn't over yet!' There was a blur in the doorway that might have been anything, and then the screen overloaded again for a few seconds.

The Doctor disappeared back into the console. This was his chance to disconnect the faulty component and reassign its functions.

'She's still got a chance,' the Doctor said.

'Doesn't that depend on where you sent her?' asked Tegan.

Now that the alarms were no longer sounding, it was possible to make out a regular pulsating hum that was coming from the console. 'We've locked onto some kind of spacecraft,' the Doctor said.

But Tegan wasn't listening. On the screen, the strange door was beginning to close of its own accord. The Doctor saw this and hurried out of the console room. Tegan started to follow.

'What's the rush?' Turlough said. 'I thought we were safe.'

Tegan paused for a moment; she wanted to tell him that he had the hide of an elephant. Instead she flashed him a disapproving look, and set out after the Doctor.

The new door in the far wall had completely closed. The Doctor went over to examine it, but for the moment he didn't touch. Turlough was pushing his way in from the corridor as Tegan said, 'How strong's the link?'

'We're well hooked,' the Doctor said. The door

23

wasn't really telling him anything; it was as much a part of the TARDIS as of the craft they'd contacted. On the other side, there would probably be an opening where there had been no opening before. If there was a crew to be met on the other side, he hoped they'd be flexible in their thinking.

Tegan said, 'Hadn't we better find out what we've sent Nyssa into?'

The Doctor shot her a look of impatient reproof, but it was mild. He understood that she was as anxious as he was for Nyssa's safety. His first touch of the door caused it to open automatically.

It had a wide swing and, like Nyssa, they all had to take a pace back. A metallic scent-cocktail of machine-scrubbed air came wafting through, reminding Tegan of aircraft runways and oil-stained tarmac and open bay-doors, causing a stab of nostalgia that wasn't entirely unpleasant. There wasn't much to see other than dim lights and dark metal. She said, 'Are we going through?' She was doing her best to sound confident, but she wasn't quite making it.

'*I'll* go through,' the Doctor said. 'You wait here.'

He hesitated for just a moment, and then he went to the threshold and stepped down. Tegan followed him to the edge and looked through after him.

What she saw was a section of a corridor complex formed from staggered alcoves down one side with a curving wall opposite that was probably a part of the ship's outer skin. The floor was a see-through metal grating over a cable trap, and the lighting seemed to be set at night-time levels. The Doctor was standing and looking around. The only sounds were the drone of buried motors and, laid faintly over this, an

24

ethereal windsong that was deceptively like far-off crying.

'Well?' Tegan said.

'She's gone.'

'Which way?'

The Doctor was about to say that there was no way of knowing, but then he saw something a short distance away that made him think again. He walked over for a closer look. It was a biotechnical text from the TARDIS library. It was scorched along one edge. He set it against the wall and turned back to Tegan. 'Stay back,' he said. 'She can't have gone far.' And then he set off in the direction that the book had indicated.

Tegan waited and listened when he'd gone from sight, but after a few moments the sound of his footsteps faded. They hadn't left it too long; surely Nyssa must have realised after a while that the danger was over and she could stop running. Perhaps she'd turned around and was heading back already. Tegan was doing her best to be optimistic, but she couldn't get the image of the damaged book out of her mind.

She moved back into the TARDIS. 'Nyssa's gone,' she told Turlough.

Nyssa's abacus had been warped and scorched, but otherwise it was recognisable. Turlough had picked it up, and he was flicking the beads from side to side. He said, 'The Doctor will find her.'

'Do you really care?'

Turlough was smiling. 'Do you know, Tegan,' he said, 'it wouldn't be possible for me to be the ogre you seem to think I am.'

'Really?' Tegan said, and her disbelief was obvious.

'Really. I mean, am I criticising you because you'd

rather stay here than help look for Nyssa?'

That did it. She turned and went out through the doorway.

Turlough watched for a moment in case Tegan changed her mind, but he wasn't expecting it. Of the three, she was the easiest to manipulate. All he needed to do was to annoy her a little, and she'd jump off impulsively in whatever direction he wanted. He reached into his pocket and brought out the contact cube.

Although he couldn't say so, he blamed his controller for his earlier failure. There had to be a better way of bringing the Doctor down than by striking at his technology; that, after all, was the Doctor's strength. The cube started to glow.

'They've left me alone,' Turlough said as soon as contact was established. 'What can I do?'

'Nothing. Destroying the TARDIS is nothing if the Doctor lives.'

'He's gone.'

'Then follow and kill him. Find a way.'

Tegan hadn't even gone out of sight of the door when Turlough stepped down into the corridor. It wasn't going to be as simple as it had seemed at first; the corridor branched and divided further down, and the monotony of its appearance was disorienting. She heard her name being called, and she turned back to see what he wanted.

He was walking towards her, and she saw with a start of fear that the door was closing itself behind him. No doubt it would open again when someone approached it, and if there was any problem in

26

tracking it down there was always Nyssa's book that they could use as a marker, but Tegan still felt as if a cell door had been slammed on her.

But the big surprise was Turlough. He was looking sheepish. He was *embarrassed*.

'Sorry,' he said, 'That must have looked really selfish. I couldn't let you come out here alone.'

It was certainly a change of heart, but Tegan wasn't about to take any bets on how long it might last. When she turned around to lead the way, there was that familiar uncomfortable feeling between her shoulders again.

In fact, she'd been on the point of turning back. It no longer seemed like a good idea to try to catch up with the Doctor, and it was only the thought of Turlough waiting and smirking at her lack of resolve that had caused her to hesitate, but now that he was with her and tagging along, she felt even less able to give up the notion.

So they followed the way laid down by the book, as the Doctor had done, pressing deeper into the unknown craft and walking in what they hoped were his footsteps. They paused only once, when the steady engine sounds from under the decks changed and became less intense. By then they were already some distance away from their starting point; there was no way that they might have seen their link to the TARDIS slowly fading out and leaving a blank section of corridor wall.

The Doctor was either staying well ahead of them or else he'd turned off somewhere. Tegan and Turlough moved as fast as they dared without making too much noise, staying with the main line of the corridor; this way they stood the least chance of getting lost, because they'd be able to trace a straight line back to their starting-point.

They met nobody. The place even had an empty feel about it, helped along by the low-level lights. For Tegan it was like an engine yard at midnight, and the only life was that which throbbed through the decks under their feet. Even so, this didn't make her any less uneasy – lights of any kind, even at the lowest level, must have been provided for someone to see by. There were sliding doors at regular intervals down one side of the main corridor, but none was open.

Thanks for that, at least, Tegan thought as they pressed on.

'Was that her?' Turlough said suddenly, and Tegan realised that she'd been letting her attention wander.

'What?' she said, but Turlough signed for her to be quiet.

They listened for nearly a minute, and finally it came again: what Tegan had assumed to be the far-off moaning of air through the craft's recirculation system was augmented by another, more distinctive sound. It was something very like a human cry.

'Well?' Turlough said.

Tegan listened again, but the sound wasn't repeated. 'I don't know,' she said, 'I suppose it could have been...'

But Turlough was already convinced. He even seemed to be sure of the direction, down a tunnel that intersected with the main corridor only a little way ahead. 'Come on,' he said, 'we'll catch up with the Doctor on the way.'

'Wait a minute! We could get lost!'

'All taken care of,' Turlough said, and he held

28

something out under the nearest of the dim lights. Tegan took a closer look and saw that it was the abacus.

Turlough took hold of one of the crosswires and sprung it loose from the frame. The beads ran from it easily into his hand, and he crouched. 'We'll leave a trail,' he explained, and he took one of the beads and set it in one of the cut-out squares of the floor grating. It sat neatly, too small to roll out and too big to fall through. 'All we'll have to do is follow the beads home.'

Tegan couldn't help being impressed. 'Don't miss a trick, do you?' she said.

Damn it if Turlough didn't come close to actually blushing. 'I look after myself,' he said.

Then both of them heard it, and this time there was no mistaking what it was: a girl's voice, far-off and filled with anguish. Even if Turlough hadn't already come up with a sure method of finding their way back, Tegan would probably have been unable to resist the summons. It was clear evidence that Nyssa was alive and hurt, and for Tegan there was no other explanation.

Leaving Turlough to take care of their trail, she was already heading down the tunnel.

Whatever was making the sound, Nyssa could hear it too.

It came from somewhere overhead. She crouched in the darkness below the metal stairway of the lower deck with her eyes shut, waiting for it to stop. Some of the dizziness was going but there was still the nausea whenever she tried to move, and any sound was like needles in her ears. She didn't know where she was, or how far she'd run; all that she could remember was the advancing edge of the field of instability as it devoured the room around her, and then the blinding pain and the Doctor's voice urging her to keep moving. Well, she'd kept moving even though her vision had been distorted worse than the worst of bad dreams and her head had been pounding with a dull, regular beat. She'd kept on until a measure of conscious control had returned and she'd found herself half-way down the stairs to the lower deck, clutching the rail and on the point of pitching forward.

It'll pass, she'd told herself desperately, wanting nothing more than to let herself down slowly and let the bad feelings ebb away. She made it to the bottom of the stairs, where her legs almost gave out. It was then that she'd turned and seen the shadowed area underneath, and she'd crawled into the darkness much as a beaten fox might crawl into its hole.

The wailing had started then. *Please*, someone seemed to be calling, *help me*. Even though there were no clear words, the message was plain. It was more than Nyssa could bear. After a few moments she covered her ears and did her best to sit it out.

As she rested, she started to feel better. The improvement was only relative, but at least the nausea began to subside. After a while she took her hands away from her ears and opened her eyes; even the lights no longer hurt. In a minute or so, she promised herself, she'd try to stand. As long as that far-off agony didn't start up again, Nyssa felt that she could face whatever she'd got into.

It was as she was standing that she heard a light footfall on the stairs above.

Nyssa froze, and waited. Whatever was coming

down towards her had hesitated, too, but after a moment it came on. She could see its shadow through the open construction of the stairway, and hear its weight on the metal as it descended with stealth. She held her breath.

No details, just a dark shape. It came down to deck level and turned to step out into the light. Even though she'd been determined to stand quite still – there was always the chance that it wouldn't see her, and pass on by – Nyssa couldn't help taking half a pace back into the greater safety of the darkness.

The wall behind her was closer than she'd thought. She came up against it with an almost inaudible bump... it was almost nothing, but it was enough to be heard.

'Nyssa?' the Doctor said. He was standing at the bottom of the stairway, one hand on the rail, peering uncertainly into the shadows.

For a moment she was sufficiently overcome to hug him, and he was sufficiently relieved to let her. He said, 'Where did you think you were going?'

'I had no idea,' Nyssa said, finally stepping back. She could even stand without swaying, now. 'I got all scrambled up, and I didn't know where I was going. I was just about to start looking for the way back. Where are we?'

The Doctor looked around. 'My guess is that it's some old passenger liner.'

'But where are the passengers?'

'I don't know. Let's get back.'

Tegan and Turlough had been going wrong for more than half the distance that they'd covered, but they had no way of knowing it. Tegan's preoccupation had been with speed – keep going and they'd soon overtake the Doctor – and she stayed with the idea much longer than was practical. It was because of this that she'd missed the simple clue that had taken the Doctor off down a side-branch some distance back and eventually to the lower deck where Nyssa had been hiding: the mark of Nyssa's hand, lightly printed into the dust and grime of the corridor wall as she'd reached out to support herself in turning the corner.

But now Tegan had a new preoccupation, which was to track down the source of the sound that they'd heard. In her own mind she was already convinced that it was Nyssa, and a Nyssa in severe distress at that. Every step closer that she took increased her conviction. Turlough followed, marking their trail and doing his best to keep up.

Eventually, the inevitable happened. 'We're out of beads,' he called to Tegan.

Tegan stopped and looked back. 'But we're almost there,' she said. 'I'm sure of it.'

Turlough shrugged, and showed her the empty frame. Perhaps they could break it up and use the pieces to extend the trail a little, but the difference that it could make would be negligible.

There wasn't a choice. They'd seen enough of the complex of curves and turns that made up the several decks of the liner to know that, without some system of marking the way, they'd have only the slimmest chance of finding their way back. Tegan simply couldn't argue.

'All right,' she said reluctantly, 'we'll head back and see if we can meet up with the Doctor. But leave the trail so we can follow it again.'

Now it was Turlough's turn to lead. He left the

frame against one wall as a sign of the trail's end, and they went back to the first intersection of the route back to the TARDIS. And here Turlough stopped.

Tegan looked at him; he was scanning the floor, confused, and she felt an immediate tremor of apprehension somewhere deep inside. 'What's the matter?' she said.

'It's gone.'

'What?'

Turlough pointed. 'The last of the beads. It was there.'

Tegan looked around; two other branch corridors joined close by. 'It must be one of the other sections, then,' she said, but even before she'd finished Turlough was shaking his head. There was no way he could expect to remember their entire route, but he was sure of the very last turning they'd made.

He wasn't quite so sure about the next intersection, but he set out to check with Tegan only a little way behind. She was thinking that perhaps the bead had dropped through the grating. They couldn't all be a regular size, and besides, there was no other explanation – from all that they'd seen, they were alone on a deserted ship. She and Turlough had come far enough for her to be sure that, if there had been anyone around, they'd at least have seen a sign of it. And if there was nobody to disturb the beads, it therefore didn't make sense that the beads should be disturbed...

Turlough reached the corner, and stopped abruptly. There was no more than a fraction of a second's reaction time in which he stood with amazement on his face, and then he was hustling Tegan over to the corridor wall and motioning urgently for her to be quiet.

She tried to pantomime a look of enquiry. He stepped aside so that she could take a cautious peek around the corner. His hand was on her arm, ready to pull her back if he saw unexpected danger.

There was some kind of robot, and it was picking up their beads.

It was small and battered, and no attempt had been made to mimic a humanoid shape. It was an obvious work-horse machine, a drone. From the front, its bodyshell presented an octagonal profile with diode lights and indicator panels on the forward section. Above this, in lieu of a head, was a camera housing raised on a curved gooseneck stalk. It looked like the flattened head of a snake as it scanned from side to side, searching across the flooring for anything else to collect. Folded flat against the shell were anglepoise arm mechanisms, each tipped with an evil-looking blade or drill facing forward like weapons at the ready. Two of these – both pincers – had swung out for use, one to pick up the beads and the other to hold the growing collection in a semi-transparent bag.

Satisfied that there was nothing else to be found, the drone straightened. It had probably been programmed to keep the corridors clear of any obstruction, large or small. If it had any defence function in addition to simple maintenance, neither Tegan nor Turlough wanted to find out the hard way. They watched as it turned, centred itself on its gyros, and moved off in the opposite direction. Some way down the corridor it stopped, turned, and set off again, and eventually disappeared out of sight.

And it took all their chances with it, rattling together in a semi-transparent bag.

Their names were Olvir and Kari, and they were raiders. Their entry into the liner was no less spectacular or unusual than that of the TARDIS party, and it was carried off with considerably more noise and damage.

The sequence had been well rehearsed, in simulation and on countless other real-life missions. The limited spread of the thermic charges attached on the outside instantly vapourised a ring of metal large enough for them to pass through. A high wind blew down the corridor section as air drained out through the hole and the ventilator pumps went into overload trying to replace it, and dust and debris whirled around in the vortex before the gap as the two suited figures entered.

Kari was first because she had the experience. She came through with her burner ready to fire and expecting trouble, bracing herself against the tug of the air-loss and scanning around in an even sweep. Olvir was at her back in a moment, and as the strong winds died they stood and kept both main approaches covered.

They were wearing lightweight assault gear, enough for a few minutes' resistance to vacuum without slowing them down. The close-fitting suits and the smooth pressure-helmets gave them an intimidating appearance which, after the shock of the initial entry, was usually enough to overcome any resistance.

Assuming, that was, that any kind of resistance was presented; the lack of resistance was the first thing on the liner that didn't coincide with what they'd been expecting.

The outward rush of air finally stopped. Both raiders carried hand-radios clipped alongside the spare power-packs on their belts, but assault procedure required radio silence until primary reconnaissance had been carried out. They restricted themselves instead to the low-power helmet communication that couldn't be picked up outside a circle of a few metres.

'Check the air-seal,' Kari said, and she kept watch in both directions as Olvir went back to their entry point. The hole was now plugged with what appeared to be solidified foam. Olvir spread his fingers and pushed against it, but his gloved hand barely made a dent. A few minutes longer, and the foam would have set as hard as the metal around it.

He signalled to Kari that there was no problem. A last check in both directions, and then with a jerk of her burner she indicated for him to follow as she set off down the corridor.

They'd spent six of the last twelve hours in deep hypnosis, memorising every turn of the route ahead as it was shown in plans that the Chief had bought under a false name for the servicing agents – not that this particular model appeared to have seen a service bay in more than its safe quota of runs, which was a second worrying factor.

The plan was to fight their way from the access point to the bridge, where they were to take prisoners and over-ride the airlock seals so that the main force of the raiding party could enter. It was for this that they'd fixed in their minds every scrap of cover, every firing angle, every short-cut and potential source of a hidden enemy. But *this*… this wasn't right.

The light was bad, and the corridor was grimy.

There were no guards and no defensive devices. Ever suspicious, Kari wondered if it was some kind of original approach designed to get their defences down so they could be hit without expecting it; but as they came into the last part of the run leading to the liner's control room and they'd still seen no signs of life, she was starting to discount the theory.

The doors were open. Olvir looked at her for guidance, and she signalled him in. They came through together, crouching low to reduce the target, and turned their weapons onto an empty room.

Kari straightened slowly. She no longer believed that they might be facing some kind of odd defensive strategy. What she sensed instead was a serious miscalculation. It was basically a standard control room, with tiers of crew positions facing a deep-set panoramic window that probably showed a simulation rather than a direct view of the distant stars. What made it unusual was the ugly piece of equipment under the window, obviously not a part of the original specification but grafted on. Lines and cables appeared to link this to the various crew controls, and other cables ran out to disappear under the floor grating.

Kari lowered her guard, and then, after only a moment's hesitation, she removed her pressure helmet. Following her lead, Olvir did the same.

'I don't get it,' she said.

Olvir looked around. It was his first mission as a member of an advance party, and everything was equally new to him. 'What's wrong?' he said, and as he turned towards her he made his first real mistake by bringing her into the firing area of his burner.

Kari guided the muzzle away firmly. 'The whole

37

ship's rigged to run on automatics,' she said. 'It doesn't fit the briefing.'

'Can't we open the airlocks ourselves?'

'That's not the point.' Kari walked around the forward control desk for a closer look at the odd unit, leaving Olvir to stand alone. He looked at the nearest crew positon. The read-out screen and the picture symbols on the input keys seemed to indicate a navigation console. He reached out to press the nearest of the keys, wondering what might happen.

'Don't touch anything,' Kari said sharply. She didn't even seem to be looking his way. Olvir withdrew his hand as if it had been slapped.

Kari was still looking at what was probably the automated command centre that was guiding and operating the liner. Olvir waited out the silence for a while, and finally said, 'So... what next?'

'There's atmosphere, but no crew,' Kari said, thinking aloud. 'Doors that won't open. No cargo space.' She turned unexpectedly, and fixed Olvir with a piercing stare. 'What does that mean to you?'

'No cargo?' Olvir hazarded.

Kari unclipped the radio from her belt. 'And it's supposed to be a merchant ship,' she said. 'I'm going to call the Chief.'

She opened the frequency and gave the call sign, and for a while they waited. There was no reason for the Chief not to respond. It was a part of the plan to establish contact when the bridge had been taken, but the radio stayed silent. Kari tried again.

'Bad signal?' Olvir suggested when there was still no reply, but Kari shook her head.

'It would register. Maybe it's the handset. You try.'

Olvir unclipped his own handset and gave the call

sign, not really expecting to get any different result from Kari. He didn't.

'The gear's usually reliable,' Kari said, but the thought that followed it remained unspoken: *I wish I could say the same about the Chief...*

'Chief,' she said suddenly, 'I know you're listening. It's not working out. We're coming back.'

'We can't,' Olvir pointed out, 'if he doesn't link with the airlock.' Kari looked at him then, and he saw the apprehension in her eyes. If something scared Kari, anybody else around who wasn't worried was probably seriously out of touch with the situation.

'He'd better,' she started to say, 'or...' She stopped abruptly. Voices! And coming their way!

For this, there was a procedure. Fear could wait, pushed out of the way by training and routine. Quickly she gave Olvir his orders.

No one knew more than the Doctor that they were in a difficult situation – uninvited guests in an unknown environment – but he was beginning to think that, with speed of action and a fast withdrawal, they'd be able to carry it off without too much danger. There was nobody around, they hadn't been challenged, and he was confident that he could remember the way back to the TARDIS where Tegan and Turlough would be waiting, as ordered. Considering the way events could have gone, they'd turned out well.

At least, that's what he'd thought until they came upon the plugged hole in the liner's outer skin. Suddenly he was no longer so confident. 'This is new,' he said, crossing the corridor for a closer look.

Nyssa didn't understand. 'New?'

The Doctor placed his hand on the surface of the

hardened foam, carefully at first and then with increased pressure. Solid as rock. It didn't seem likely that it could have formed in the short time since he'd first passed this way. The only other explanation was that he'd taken a wrong turn somewhere, and that they were in a new and unfamiliar part of the ship. He said to Nyssa, 'Do you remember anything at all about the way you came?'

But Nyssa shook her head. 'Nothing. I didn't know where I was going, or what I was doing. I just ran as you told me to.'

He touched the foam again. It wasn't even warm. Well, he told himself, when you're offered a choice of explanations you have to pick the simplest, unless there's some good reason not to. And right now, there's no good reason to suppose we're anything other than... well, not lost, just a little way off the beam.

'We're on the right level, anyway,' he said, doing his best not to communicate any more anxiety to Nyssa. She'd already been through enough. He pointed back down the corridor and said, 'It'll be this way.'

They started to move back. They were on the right level and in the main corridor, so it was really only a matter of time before they came across the TARDIS. The slight curve of the passageway suggested that, if they were to go on for long enough, they might eventually return to their starting-point – in which case they had nothing to worry about. All they had to do was to keep going, and they'd cover the entire ship.

But the corridor didn't make a circuit. After a few minutes of walking and not finding the TARDIS, they came to the corridor's end and an open door. They hesitated long enough to make sure that the area ahead wasn't holding any nasty surprises for them, and then they went through.

'This has got to be the control room,' the Doctor explained, looking around. 'With any luck, we can find out where we are from here.'

The Doctor was no stranger to other people's spacecraft, and he already had a reasonable idea of what to expect. Societies with limited experience and expertise in space travel tend to produce short-hop craft of restricted capability and with control systems that look as if they would take a lifetime of study to master. More developed cultures tend towards a high level of automation, with simplified controls and, as often as not, some indication of their use that isn't tied to a single language or set of languages. The long-haul liner obviously fell into the second category. Attempting to get some sense out of the inboard computers would be feasible, even if it was time wasting and tedious, but what the Doctor had in mind was something simpler. He wanted to check around the walls for a floor plan of the liner.

He didn't get the chance. As he and Nyssa approached the control desk, someone rose up from behind it and levelled a weapon at them. He was youngish, hardly more than a boy.

The Doctor quickly steered Nyssa around, saying, 'Sorry, didn't know it was private.' But their exit was already blocked. The rifle-like burner in the girl's hand came down to cover them, and she looked fully capable of using it.

'That's all right,' she said. 'We're in a mood for company.'

But somehow, the Doctor didn't feel that he could

41

believe her.

'This makes twice in one day,' Turlough said as they hesitated at yet another junction of corridors. Every direction seemed the same. They hadn't even managed to find their way back to the main thoroughfare, and now they were having to move slowly because of the need to check for any robot drones that might be heading their way.

Tegan didn't understand. 'What do you mean?'

'You lost your way in the TARDIS, as well.'

'If it wasn't for your bright idea with the beads, we'd never have come this far.'

'Arguing won't get us out of here.'

'Maybe,' Tegan said, 'but it helps my temper.' The annoying part about it was that he was right.

There were no more drones, so they took a guess and moved on. They'd seen one more of the robots, with a different coloured bodyshell and a different set of tools. It had crossed their path some way ahead and had paid them no attention. This wasn't really enough to make them feel safe – it only meant that, at the time, whatever they'd been doing hadn't raised any objection from its programming. Let them wander into some unmarked but proscribed area, and the reaction might be different.

The plaintive calling that had lured them down had stopped shortly after they'd tried to turn back. Tegan was doing her best not to think about it. But she could hardly put it from her mind when it started again – not when it was coming from the other side of a door that was only a few metres behind them.

It came through as a distinct *Help me*. Tegan was transformed; she rushed to the door and pressed her

42

head against it to listen. 'That's her,' she said, 'that's Nyssa!'

Turlough wasn't so sure. Even though they hadn't known where they were heading, they'd come a long way from their turn-around point, a place where they'd supposedly been getting near to the source. 'That could have been anybody,' he said, but Tegan was already convinced.

'Nyssa?' she said loudly, doing her best to make herself heard through the thickness of the door. 'Nyssa, are you there?'

A faint but unmistakable response came through. Tegan looked around at Turlough in triumph, as if she'd had absolute confirmation.

'It's the Doctor we have to find,' he was starting to say, but Tegan wasn't even listening.

'See?' she said. 'We've got to get the door open!'

Whilst Tegan was trying to find a way to open a sliding door that has no handle and no visible controls on the outside, the Doctor and Nyssa were sitting in two of the crew chairs in the control room of the liner. Weapons covered them from both sides, and the raiders with the weapons obviously knew how to use them.

It hadn't taken long for the Doctor to add an empty liner to a foam-plugged hole and work out how the newcomers came to be here. What he couldn't answer quite so easily was the question *why*? In the meantime, he could see no advantage either in lying or in concealing his own motives for being on the liner.

'You've got a ship?' Kari said at the first mention of the TARDIS. 'Where is it?'

43

'That's the problem,' the Doctor said. 'We can't find it.'

'Is it armed?'

The Doctor and Nyssa both spoke together. 'No,' they said, and then exchanged a glance. They wanted to present themselves neither as potential enemies nor as allies to be pressed into service. The Doctor added, 'We're not looking for trouble, we're just passing through.'

Kari turned her weapon slightly and flicked a switch on its side. The movement seemed to be as much for their benefit as for any practical purpose. The burner emitted a high-pitched whine, and a red indicator light blinked alongside the switch. She flicked it off, and the whine stopped.

'I'm not convinced,' she said.

'This is all very one-sided,' the Doctor objected.

'I know.'

Olvir's attention, meanwhile, had drifted from them and was now directed more towards the panoramic window at the forward end of the bridge. 'Kari,' he said, and the undertone of warning caused her to glance his way. It was then that she saw the moving shadows around one of the ports, the first indication of an approaching light-source somewhere outside.

'Watch them,' she said to Olvir, and she crossed over to the window to take a look.

The Doctor had already weighed the possibility of making a run for it, and dismissed the idea. Olvir might be number two in the raider hierarchy, but he still knew what he was doing. Even if they made it out into the corridor, they'd be perfect targets. From his seat by what was probably the liner's manual helm,

44

the Doctor watched as Kari stared out at something they couldn't see. She seemed to be getting paler and paler, all of her colour bleaching away until she had to turn aside from the brightness or be blinded. The windowglass reacted a moment later, darkening in response to the photon overload as a deep rumble made itself felt all the way through the control room.

Olvir couldn't help it. He had to see. He continued to keep the Doctor and Nyssa within his firing arc as he backed over to the window but he switched his attention away from them for a moment. Nyssa looked at the Doctor, but the Doctor shook his head.

'That's our ship!' Olvir said in disbelief.

Kari had unclipped her radio from her belt and was making a hasty attempt to communicate. 'Chief,' she said, 'this is the advance party. What's happening?'

But Olvir had already guessed. It was the obvious sequel to the lack of follow-up and the long radio silence – a silence which even now wasn't to be broken. 'He's running out on us!' he said.

'He can't!' Kari tried again, but her only reply was a deafening wash of static as the raid ship's engines burned their way past. She switched off. The quiet of deep space was abruptly back with them, the only background sounds those of the liner's engines running themselves up in preparation for some automated manoeuvre.

The Doctor leaned fractionally towards Nyssa. She looked at him, eager to hear the plan of action that would get them out of this mess.

'Any ideas?' he said.

'It's the motors,' Turlough said as he stepped back from the door, and he listened for a moment to be certain. 'Something's happening.'

Tegan didn't even seem to hear. They'd found that, by pressing hard and putting all of their strength into it, they could make the door give just a little. It wasn't enough to be of any real use, but it looked like progress. She said, 'Hold on, Nyssa, we're getting you out.'

Turlough had his own reasons for being helpful. His sights were set, not on Nyssa, but on the Doctor. Helping Tegan was only a way of keeping his cover intact whilst he waited for the opportunity that the Black Guardian had assured him would come. He said, 'We need a crowbar. Something to lever the door open.'

'Well, find one!'

That's easy to say, he thought, *but where*? Tegan was ignoring him, pressing all around the frame as she searched for weak spots. There might be an easier way out. What if he presented himself to the Doctor as the only survivor? Tegan had followed him out and he, Turlough, had tried to dissuade her. It had been no use. He'd called to her and after a while he'd followed her. An open door and a deep airshaft, with maybe a conclusive piece of evidence like a scrap of material caught on the edge... he knew he could make it sound convincing. He could strike now, while all of Tegan's attention was on the door.

Tegan stopped. She turned as if he'd touched her and she stared at him. *She knows*, he thought, *somehow she senses it*. 'I'm on my way,' he said, backing off. She watched him all the way to the corner.

The engine sounds were much louder here, drumming their way up through the open flooring. He

46

didn't think that there was much chance of finding anything that resembled a crowbar, but he had to make a show. From now on he would have to try twice as hard to convince Tegan that he was above board, or she'd be watching him so closely that he'd never have an opportunity to get near to the Doctor.

Assuming that he needed one. The more Turlough thought about it, the more it seemed that his best opportunity had already been handed to him. His controller had been so quick to order him outside that he hadn't waited to hear the details of the situation. Take the TARDIS away and the Doctor would be helpless, marooned, as good as dead ... and it could be carried off without personal risk to Turlough.

This would be an ideal time to set the plan in motion. It was as he was reaching into his pocket for the contact cube that Turlough saw Nyssa's book.

It was against the wall, just as the Doctor had left it – except then it had been within a few metres of the link to the TARDIS. The door itself was gone. In its place was metal plating that showed no sign of ever having been disturbed.

'Turlough!' Tegan called from around the corner. 'It's moving!'

'I'm on my way,' he replied, but he made no move to return. Instead he approached the book. It might have been reasonable to suppose that a passing drone might clear it away as so much litter, but that it should be moved to some other location and placed in exactly the same way would be too bizarre to be expected.

There was only one conclusion: this was the place, but the link to the TARDIS had faded away.

'I could use some help!' Tegan called, and now there was an edge of real annoyance in her voice.

'I'm coming,' Turlough said, with as much intention of carrying this out as before. The throb of the liner's motors had increased so much that it was now shaking the corridor floor. There was also something rather more interesting that was starting to happen.

The TARDIS was coming back.

First came the shadows, then the details. The massive door sketched itself in quickly, and then this was followed by a slower filling-out. Turlough was about to call to Tegan, but then he checked himself and smiled. Wasn't this exactly what he'd wanted? He took a step forward, feeling the floor shiver as the liner's engines strained and altered their pitch.

And then, the door began to die away. It was a ghost again before it had even managed to become solid, and then it was gone completely.

He'd been so close! The door had been starting to open for him! Just a couple more seconds and he'd have been inside and on his way. He made a fist and slammed it against the wall in frustration – there was no give, and he almost damaged himself.

So now it was back to the original plan, ingratiate and subvert. It would be a lot more difficult, but now he didn't have any choice. Tegan had been silent for a while. She was probably angry at him, and his first job would be to get her confidence back. He looked at his skinned knuckles, and they gave him an idea.

He came back around the corner holding his wrist and making a good show of somebody who's hurt but is trying to ignore the pain. What he saw made him forget the strategy.

Whatever Tegan had managed to release, it wasn't Nyssa – and it was pinning her to the door.

A hand wrapped in bandages was over her mouth,

and another had a hold on her wrist. The door had been pushed back no more than a few inches, but whatever was behind was now trying to open it further. Turlough stood with an expression of dazed wonder at the scene, but then Tegan managed to shake away the bent claw that covered her face for long enough to shout, 'Don't just *watch*!'

He dived forward, and grabbed the arm before it could get another grip. It quickly withdrew, leaving him with a momentary but unforgettable impression of scales and dirty linen. Tegan tried to pull herself away from the claw that was hooked around her wrist, and Turlough beat at it until it let go. It snapped back as if on a spring, and the door slammed shut.

There were scrabbling sounds for a while, but they died down. After a few moments of silence, the wailing started again; it no longer sounded anything like Nyssa. It didn't even sound like anything human.

'You took your time,' Tegan said resentfully. She was rubbing at her arm, as if she'd never be able to get it clean.

'I found the doorway to the TARDIS.'

The transformation of Tegan's mood was immediate. 'Where?'

'It's gone again.'

'What do you mean?'

'The bridge is only temporary. We're in worse trouble than we thought.'

Tegan eyed the sliding panel, with the horror-show behind it. How many similar doors had they passed in their wandering through the liner? She said, 'You're saying that we can't go back.'

Turlough considered for a moment. 'It seems that way,' he said. 'So I think the most important thing for us to do now is to find the Doctor, don't you?'

Find the Doctor. Then wait for the right moment.

'But why run out?' Olvir said for the second time. It went against everything he'd been taught.

Kari had been given the opportunity to see rather more of the Chief's tactics in the field. 'We won't be the first party he's dumped,' she said. 'He's found out something he didn't know before, and suddenly we're expendable.'

Olvir looked towards the Doctor and Nyssa. His burner was still trained in their direction, and he'd made them both spread their hands on the console before them so he'd have warning of any attempts to move. The Doctor seemed to be taking an interest in the console read-outs. Olvir said, 'And what about them? Where do they fit in?'

Kari dismissed them with a glance. 'They're harmless,' she said. 'But we can use their ship.'

Nyssa was keeping her voice almost to a whisper, so that their captors wouldn't hear. 'Where do you think *they* fit in?' she said.

'Raiders, by the sound of it,' he said. 'You know, kind of high-technology pirates. They'll be a small advance party sent in to open the airlocks for the main forces.'

'But raiding what?'

Nyssa was right. There seemed to be nothing about the liner that was worth a raider's attention. Olvir and Kari were obviously as surprised by this as anyone. The Doctor said, 'Perhaps they were misinformed.'

The two of them were now on their way over. Kari hefted her burner, just in case it needed bringing to the Doctor's attention again, and said, 'You're taking

50

us away from here.'

The Doctor's reply was fast and firm. 'Not at the point of a gun.'

'I'm not giving you a choice.'

'And I'm not giving you a lift.'

Kari took a step closer. 'I don't have to kill you. I could hurt one of you very badly.'

'And blow the last chance you've got.' The Doctor indicated the range of information displays before him. 'You don't have to be a genius to understand what these things are saying, just listen to the engines. Those are alignment manoeuvres. We're docking with something.'

Olvir came to stand behind Kari's shoulder. 'It could be what scared the Chief away,' he said.

The Doctor pressed his opportunity. 'We'll take you,' he said. 'But it's a truce or nothing.'

Olvir was looking at Kari. After a moment, she nodded. They turned their weapons aside.

From now on, the Doctor believed, it ought to be easy. He told himself afterwards that he should have known better.

He was sure that his earlier ideas on how to find the way home had been correct. The discovery of the raiders' entry point had made him think otherwise, but now it should simply be a case of back-tracking to some recognisable stage of the journey, and then proceeding as before. Kari seemed wary about this, but Nyssa reassured her. 'The Doctor knows what he's doing,' she said, and then she turned away quickly. She didn't want any of her own doubts to show – after all, he *had* just rescued her, but she knew of old that the Doctor tended to sail into the darkest situations with a seamless display of confidence.

The first recognisable stage of the journey turned out to be the stairs to the lower deck where he'd found Nyssa – at least, they looked like the stairs, even though to the others they seemed no different to any of three that they'd already passed.

'We can't go wrong from here,' the Doctor said after he'd descended a couple of steps to check around, and it was as he turned back to rejoin the others that the lights came on.

Olvir and Kari immediately reached for their weapons. The night-time levels of both decks were turning into an artificial dawn, and the change had come without any warning. The effect was almost painful to their darkness-tuned eyes, and by some strange inversion the liner had suddenly become more threatening. The ship no longer slept.

There was more. It spoke to them.

Concealed speakers down the length of every corridor crackled and came alive. The voice that boomed around them was slurred and inhuman.

'*All decks stand by,*' it echoed. Olvir and Kari were scanning around in every direction, tensed for any attack. '*All decks stand by. This is a special announcement from Terminus Incorporated. Primary docking alignment procedures are now complete. Passengers with mobility should prepare to disembark …*'

Some distance away and heading in completely the wrong direction, Tegan and Turlough stopped to listen in awe.

'*Anyone failing to disembark will be removed. Sterilisation procedures will follow. Chances of surviving the sterilisation procedures are low.'*

They looked at one another. It sounded grim, and they'd already thought that matters were as bad as they could get, but still there was more.

Tegan put her hand on Turlough's arm. He didn't need her to direct his attention, because he could see for himself: all around them, doors were beginning to slide.

They'd already seen as much as they ever wanted to see of what lay behind. Their shared urge was to run ... but where? There were doors in every corridor, and corridors on every deck, and no way of knowing for sure how many decks there were. As they backed away the entire liner seemed to have become a single, living entity, and the blistering heat of its attention was being brought around to bear on them.

Kari didn't like it any better. If she was going to have an enemy, she also wanted a target. 'Who *is* that?' she said.

'Recorded message,' the Doctor guessed. 'Automated, like everything else.'

The automated voice ground on. *'There is no return. This is your Terminus.'*

In case anybody had missed it, an electronic repeat picked up the message. *Terminus, Terminus*, it droned, over and over.

It meant nothing to the Doctor, and it didn't seem to mean anything to Nyssa. It certainly didn't mean anything to Kari... but Olvir's jaw dropped in sudden understanding.

Terminus, the repeat said as Olvir shifted his uneasy grip on his burner and took a couple of steps back. *Terminus*, as he turned away. *Terminus*, as he broke into a panicky, desperate run back in the direction of the liner control room.

'Olvir!' Kari shouted, but despite the edge of command in her voice he didn't stop.

'I think I know what's happening here!' he called back over his shoulder, and a moment later he was out of sight.

The Doctor looked at the others. 'That's knowledge that ought to be shared,' he said, and without any need for discussion the group set off after him.

They'd barely covered half the distance, when the doors around them began to open.

The Doctor saw this first, and he halted the party. There was no way of knowing what lay ahead, but he had a feeling that they were about to find out.

The electronic voice droned on. After a few moments, the first of the figures emerged. Then came another. Then came a hundred.

They flooded out, shuffling and swaying and filling the corridor like a sudden tide. They were bent and lame and mostly in rags, and most of the rags were filthy. Many faces were covered, some by muslin hoods through which only a dim shadow of features could be seen. Others were bareheaded, with bone-white skin that contrasted with dark eyes and lips. They moved in silence, pressing and crowding and jostling towards the three, some groping blindly and some leaning on those next to them – an army of the living dead.

The Doctor held out his arms to motion the others back. Nobody argued, but when he looked over his shoulder he could see that the corridor behind them offered no chance of passage. It was filled wall to wall with the half-decayed and the dying, a mighty sea of unspeaking disease that was even now on the move to close in around them. There was nowhere to go, nowhere to run, and as they pressed into one of the recesses formed by the shape of the corridor they knew that it was no cover at all.

And over the heads of this army of the lost came Olvir's voice, echoing through the ship. '*Well,*' he was shouting, '*now we know, don't we?*'

In the doorway to the control room, he gripped the frame and bellowed as loudly as he could. Behind him the automated systems of the liner ticked on without noticing. 'We know what scared the Chief away,' he yelled, and then he looked over his shoulder. The vista that had been rising across the panoramic window as the liner coasted in for its final docking now filled it from side to side. 'We're at the Terminus, where all the Lazars come to die.' Spotlights from the liner played over the passing sides of the Terminus ship, huge, dark and forbidding. Slowly, through one of the beams passed an immense rendering of a screaming skull, one of the most potent warnings to be found in any sector.

The meaning behind his next words came over clearly to the others. His voice was shot through with the despair of the already defeated.

'*We're on a leper ship!*'

The Doctor could think of plenty of news that he'd rather receive. He wasn't familiar with any disease that went by the name used by Olvir, but the evidence for its existence was all around them and pressing closer.

'Don't let them touch you,' he told Nyssa. One of the figures was getting dangerously near.

Nyssa pulled back as far as she could, almost flattening herself into the angle formed by the corridor walls. 'I wasn't thinking of it,' she said.

The Doctor's attention returned to the Lazars. They seemed to be shuffling along blindly and without volition, obeying some deeply implanted impulse that had perhaps been drummed into them at an earlier time: *when the voice speaks, everybody out*. If the three of them could simply keep out of the way, the crowd might even pass them by without any contact.

Somehow, he couldn't feel reassured. They'd been walking around, touching, breathing the air. To hope that they'd managed to avoid infection would be like standing in the rain and hoping to walk home dry.

'Excuse me,' Kari said, business-like. The Doctor began to move aside for her without thinking, but then he saw her raise the burner and level it at the nearest Lazars.

'Nyssa!' he said quickly, and Nyssa got the message right away. Standing directly alongside Kari, she clasped her hands together and drove an elbow into the raider's ribs. Kari folded instantly, her eyes wide with surprise as she gasped for breath, and the Doctor was able to reach for the burner and take it away without any resistance.

'It's all right,' he told them. 'Just hold back here, and we'll be safe. Most of them can't even see us.'

The Lazars shuffled on by, intent on some far-off goal that no observer could understand. As soon as Kari could breathe again, she said with indignation, 'You took my gun away!'

The Doctor glanced down at the burner as if he'd forgotten it. 'Oh, yes,' he said, and offered it back.

Kari took the weapon, but it was almost as if having

it taken away from her so easily had shaken some of the magic out of it. 'But we made a deal,' she protested.

'Mass slaughter wasn't a part of it.'

'Sometimes it's the only way.'

'But not this time. Look at them.'

So Kari looked. The crowd was thinning out now as the last of them went by. One was tottering blindly and holding onto the rags of the Lazar in front. A few stragglers, and then the three were able to step back into the main part of the corridor.

Nyssa said, 'What about Olvir?'

'He ran,' Kari said with unexpected harshness. 'We leave him.'

'I don't think so,' the Doctor said. 'He's got a lot to tell us.' He moved over to check the nearest of the rooms that lay beyond the now-open doors. It was empty and almost featureless, a few low benches around the walls and a mechanised water-dispenser in the middle for those who could use it. There was nothing for comfort and no sign of any emergency crash-protection, a minimum of expense for a cargo that couldn't complain. The room wasn't too clean, either.

He stepped out into the corridor and started to lead the way back towards the control room and Olvir. An embarrassed-looking Kari was the last to follow.

Tegan and Turlough were watching the last of the Lazars go past from an unusual hiding-place. After Tegan's experience at the sliding door there had been no question of them stepping aside and hoping that confrontation would pass them by, but as they'd tried to run they'd realised that it was hopeless. There was no escape at all. Every way they turned, they saw Lazars.

It was then that Turlough had started to stamp around on the metal floor. Tegan looked at him as if he'd lost his mind, but when he explained what he was doing she started to do the same.

The floor grating was laid in sections. It was Tegan who found what they needed, a loose section that rocked slightly when weight was transferred from one corner to another, and when the discovery was made they both knelt and, locking their fingers through the cross-hatched gaps in the metal, tried to heave it up from its supporting pillars.

Even though it wasn't fixed, it was heavy. At first it seemed hopeless but then, as they could hear the Lazars only metres away around the next corner, they managed to raise the grating a few inches. They were so surprised at their own success that they nearly let it fall, but desperation gave them strength. The section hinged up, and Turlough held it clear as Tegan scrambled under.

The cable-trap underneath was a shallow passageway filled with dust and grime. Tegan crouched low as Turlough followed her in and let the overhead panel drop into place. They were in relative darkness and surrounded by conduit and piping, but they could still see up into the corridor through the floor. It was a strange perspective, and one that made them feel less than safe.

The Lazars came, blotting out the light like slow-moving thunderclouds. Their rag-bound feet made a muffled pounding on the metal, and the darkness that they brought made Tegan aware of some dim sources of light down there in the channel with them – a phosphorescent build up around a corroded joint in some piping, or a neon glow escaping from behind some badly fitted safety cover.

It seemed to take forever. In amongst the Lazars was the occasional drone, supporting one who couldn't walk or leading one who couldn't see. The weight of the robots made the flooring bend and creak, and Tegan and Turlough couldn't help shrinking back slightly whenever one of them went over.

But eventually, it was over. The last of them disappeared, and there was silence. Even so, the two of them waited for a while, listening to the quiet in order to be sure. They heard a couple of clangs and bumps, but they were a long way off.

'Time to get out of here,' Tegan said and Turlough, having no reason to disagree, straightened up as much as he was able and put his shoulders against the grating to lift it.

This part ought to be so much easier, Tegan was thinking, because they were on the side where leverage could now work in their favour. But Turlough strained and pushed, and nothing happened.

'It's stuck,' he gasped finally.

'It *can't* be,' Tegan said, suppressing her panic. This was like something from the worst dream she could ever have. She added her own efforts and the two of them pushed together, and still the section wouldn't move. They both fell back, breathless.

'We'll have to find another way out,' Tegan said.

Turlough looked at the shadows around them. 'Where?'

'We'll have to look, won't we?'

They took a moment longer to recover, and then

Tegan crawled around in an attempt to find them a way through. The cable trap went wherever the corridor went, so in theory they ought to be able to follow it and keep trying the floor panels until they found another that they could raise – assuming that they hadn't all been stamped down as firmly as the one overhead. That was the theory, but the practice wasn't so straightforward. Pipes and angles and intruding shafts blocked the way, and they were going to have to do a lot of wriggling and squeezing.

As Tegan turned around, she nudged a piece of plating. It wasn't even fixed in place, and as it fell loose a greenish light came spilling from behind it. Tegan scrambled back immediately.

'It isn't even decently shielded!' she said. 'This place is a deathtrap!'

They stayed well away from the leakage, and managed to push some loose wiring aside to make a gap. The wire hadn't been disturbed in so long that the dust lay like a carpet over it. They came through into an area where they could at least move more freely, but every section they tried to lift was as firm as the last. The channel got narrower and narrower, and it ended in a blank metal wall.

'Oh, no,' Tegan said.

Turlough peered past her. 'Is there any way through?'

'Not a chance.' She knocked twice on the metal. It was like the side of a tank.

'Then we'll have to go back.'

Tegan wasn't happy at the idea, but it seemed that they didn't have any choice. She looked around into the darkness.

'Wait a minute,' she said, and stretched her hand

out to the side. It met nothing.

She pulled herself over for a look. What she'd taken to be a solid side-wall was actually the access to a vertical tunnel. Her head emerged into it and she could see that it was wide enough to take them. There were climbing-rungs all the way down, dusty but firm – as she found when she reached out and tested her weight on the nearest.

Tegan looked over her shoulder. 'We're still in business!' she said. Her voice echoed down the shaft. It almost seemed to be mocking her.

'He isn't here,' Nyssa said.

So much was obvious. The newly raised lighting levels showed an empty control room, from the panoramic window facing forward to the circuit racks at the back. Kari said, 'I told you, we leave him.'

The Doctor didn't answer immediately. He went over to the window and looked out at the part of the Terminus that was visible from their restricted angle of view. Not much showed beyond the liner's searchlights, but it seemed huge; he could see an edge of stars in only one direction.

He said, 'Leave him? That's a hard set of rules to live by.'

But Kari was unrepentant. 'He knows it.'

The Doctor studied the Terminus for a moment longer, and then he turned away from the window. It hadn't told him much, but he'd noted that the screaming skull painted across the plates seemed to be a fairly recent addition. He said, 'We didn't have any choice about coming here. What about you?'

Kari shrugged. 'It was a big liner from a rich sector. It looked like a perfect target.' She went on to explain

61

how the Chief had fixed on the liner and tracked it for some time, observing a number of pick-ups from worlds noted for their wealth and influence. When a covert research team had been sent out to check into the liner's background, they'd found exactly nothing. Officially, the liner didn't exist. The attraction of a secret cargo was irresistible to the Chief, and he'd prepared his plans and stayed on its trail until it had reached this unpatrolled area.

Well, now they'd found their secret cargo. The liner didn't look such a prize from the inside.

The Doctor said, 'And what about the Terminus?'

'I don't know. Ask Olvir, he seemed to have all the information.'

It was Nyssa who suggested that they should try to tap the liner's computer, and the Doctor agreed. All of the crew points had terminal screens and a limited array of inputs, but one place on the console seemed better served than any of the others. The Doctor guessed that it was probably the navigation desk.

The keyboard was, as he'd expected, unfamiliar, but it appeared to have been set up on principles that were mathematically rather than linguistically based. Alongside this was a row of slots, and by these a stack of rectangular plastic blocks. The blocks were loose, and they seemed to fit into the receiving spaces in any orientation.

Kari was silent at first, but the Doctor didn't seem to mind conversation. He could talk and work at the same time, neither distracting him from the other, so she leaned on the console and told him what she knew about Olvir. It wasn't much. This had been their first teaming... in fact, it had been Olvir's first mission. The rumours were that he was from a wealthy family that had gone broke, and that Olvir had saved them from ruin by contracting himself to the Chief, securing them an initial sum as an advance against his bonuses.

'So the Chief paid Olvir's family for the contract and put him straight into training,' she concluded. 'His first time out, and he messes it up.'

The Doctor had so far managed to get the liner's computer to recognise that someone was trying to communicate with it, but not much more. He said, 'And now you want to dump him.'

'That's how it goes.'

'You didn't say that when your "Chief" did it to you.'

Kari had no ready reply. Instead, she changed the subject. She indicated the screen where random graphs and patterns were rolling through, and said, 'Do you know what you're doing?'

'No.' The Doctor removed one of the blocks and inserted another. They seemed to contain coded areas of memory. 'I don't know the design and I don't know the control programme. Even if there's information about the Terminus in one of these units, I couldn't get it out.'

'So why waste time?'

'Sometimes you hit lucky. But I'd settle for a floor plan of this place.' He looked up. 'Nyssa?'

Nyssa was over by the ugly-looking box that seemed to be the source of the liner's automated control. She straightened up to see what the Doctor wanted, and he held up one of the blocks. 'Can you see any more of these?' he said, and Nyssa nodded and moved out to look.

Kari sorted through the others on the desk, looking for any sign or symbol that might distinguish one from another. 'A floor plan?' she said.

'I need to know why I got it so wrong. I remembered every turn and we still didn't find the TARDIS.'

Kari reached over and slotted in the last of the available blocks. 'Try this,' she suggested, and the Doctor typed in the limited code that he'd so far been able to devise for display.

The screen showed what was obviously a schematic diagram of several star systems, named and numbered in some unfamiliar language. 'What's that?' Kari said, indicating a zigzag dotted line that went through the systems.

'Us,' the Doctor said. The line showed every stage of the ship's journey so far. It ended in a pulsing red point that was presumably the site of the Terminus. He considered the picture for a while. Although the names were strange, he thought he could vaguely recognise the pattern that they made. He carried out a simple operation that would increase the scale, and he watched as more information came crowding in from the edges.

'What do you make of that?' he said.

'I'm combat section,' Kari replied, almost automatically. 'I don't read charts.'

Nyssa was engaged in what she believed would turn out to be a no-hope mission ... but then it was the Doctor who had asked for it, and she had more than enough reasons to be grateful to him.

The area at the back of the control room was cluttered and shadowy, with tall banks of equipment and racks of electrical relays taking up most of the space. She stood in the narrow gap between two of these and took a deep breath. Just as she thought that she'd more or less recovered, she'd get an all-over tremor and her stomach would try to do a flip. She closed her eyes and waited it out, and in a few moments it passed. It wouldn't do to let the others see; they had problems enough already. By the time she'd checked out the area behind the racks, she'd be back to normal. It was on the way to do this that she almost fell over Olvir.

He was sitting on the floor in a shadowed area, hugging his knees like a child hiding in a closet. He looked up sharply when Nyssa called his name, but then he turned his face to the darkness again.

She crouched by him, and tried not to make it sound as if she was talking to a child. That would be all that it would take to finish off his damaged pride. 'Come and talk to the Doctor,' she urged.

He wouldn't even face her. 'Forget it,' he said. 'We're dead.'

'You can't be sure.'

'This place is full of disease. We're *breathing* it.'

'It's not hopeless. We need your help.'

Nyssa waited, and after a moment Olvir unwound a little. He said, hesitantly, 'Is Kari there?'

She nodded. He thought it over for what seemed like an age, the turmoil running through him like a blade. Then he started to get to his feet.

The Doctor and Kari were still hunched over the display screen at the navigation console as they emerged from the racks. Both looked up in surprise as Olvir said loudly, 'Whatever you're planning, forget it. There's no escape.'

Kari frowned, as if she was in the habit of disbelieving news that made any situation out to be hopeless. She said, 'I've never heard of any Lazar disease.'

'There are more polite names for it,' Olvir said as he came around the end of the control desk.

The Doctor said, 'How much do you know?'

'My sister died of it. We sold everything to send her to the Terminus, but she died before she made the trip. Terminus Incorporated wouldn't return the money. We were ruined.'

Kari seemed genuinely shocked. 'I thought that was because of the fire storms on Hagen.'

'You don't advertise the Lazar disease,' Olvir said grimly.

The Doctor tapped the edge of the console thoughtfully. 'And what *is* the Terminus?'

'They talk about a cure. But I never met anyone who came back.'

But if it's such a shameful process, they'd never tell you, the Doctor was thinking, but instead of saying so he moved aside so that Olvir would be able to see the navigation screen. 'Tell me what you make of this,' he said.

'I'm combat section,' Olvir started to reply automatically, 'I don't ...' but the Doctor waved him down.

'All right. It's an expanded chart showing the position of the Terminus.'

Olvir did his best to appear interested, but he couldn't keep it up. The screen showed a vague, cloudy sphere made up of points with individual details too small to make out. At the centre of this pulsed the red point that had marked the Terminus from the beginning. He shook his head and said, 'Don't waste your time on that old hulk.'

The Doctor rarely became impatient, but he seemed to be getting close to it now. He said, 'We don't know what kind of technology may be preserved in that "old hulk".'

It was Nyssa who defused the argument before it could begin. 'But, Doctor,' she said, stepping through for a closer look at the illuminated chart, 'if that's what I think it is ...' The Doctor was nodding, encouraging her. 'Then it means that the Terminus is at the exact centre of the known universe!'

'It's all going wrong.'

'The Doctor still lives?'

'I haven't even seen him yet. I'm trapped with one of the others.'

'Because you disobeyed me.'

'I know. I'm sorry.'

'A poor beginning to your service.'

'I never killed anybody before.'

'There are weapons all around you. Keep one close to hand. Make them trust you and then, when it is least expected, strike.'

'I will.'

'You know the rewards for success. I have other rewards for your failure.'

The light in the cube began to die, as Tegan's voice came echoing through the shaft to him. 'Turlough? Is something wrong?'

He returned the cube to his pocket and leaned out over the drop. 'I'm on my way,' he called in reply, and he reached for the first of the rungs to begin his descent.

When he reached the bottom of the shaft, Turlough

67

emerged into an underfloor area that was hardly different from the one that they'd left behind. Tegan was already trying alone to raise the overhead grille, but she didn't seem to be having much success. She gave up as Turlough sat beating the dust from his clothes, and said, 'What kept you?'

'Out of practice,' Turlough said, and he glanced at the grille. 'Any luck?'

Tegan shook her head. 'Solid. I don't even think that two of us could move it.'

'Well, give me a minute and I'll ...'

But Tegan was suddenly gripping his arm so hard that he stopped before he could finish. The intent to warn was obvious. She was staring upward, and he followed the look.

The corridor above seemed no different from any other that they'd seen, with the exception that the lights were brighter down at the far end. It was a part of the liner that they hadn't covered – they knew as much because it was two or three decks down, and until the discovery of the shaft they hadn't descended at all. Now, Turlough could make out what Tegan had seen.

The lights were brighter because the corridor ended in a door to the outside. The door was open, and somebody was coming in.

He was Death.

The image occurred to Tegan straight away, and it persisted even as he strode towards them and overhead. It was impossible to tell if he was a man or a machine under the weight of the dark armour that he wore. What appeared to be the lines of bones and sinews were moulded into its surface like old brass, and around his shoulders was a heavy cloak that

68

almost reached the ground. They could feel a cold downdraft as it swept across the grating above. He carried a metal staff that lightly touched the floor with every other step. It sounded like the polite tap of the undertaker, with the carriage and the black-plumed horses waiting outside.

Both Tegan and Turlough huddled down and tried to make themselves as small as possible. They didn't even dare to breathe; dust was still thick in the air, and a single sound would have given them away. The terror of the Lazars had been bad enough, but now *this* ...

There was a drone waiting at the other end of the corridor. They saw the dark man bend to touch some kind of code into the machine's front display panel, and when he straightened they heard him speak, a single word as harsh as a saw cutting through skin:

'*Sterilise.*'

Then he turned and headed back for the door, and they closed their eyes tight as Death passed over. Again they felt the downdraft, again the slow tapping like the hammering of the Calvary nails.

'It can't get worse,' Tegan whispered, feeling as if she would burst, 'it *can't.*'

Turlough put a reassuring hand on her arm. He did it without thinking, and he surprised himself. Friendship was no part of his orders, and he'd kept it firmly out of his mind ... but such things, it seemed, were not open to conscious control.

And as he tried to pass on strength that he wasn't even sure he had, Turlough was certain of only one thing. Tegan was wrong. It could get worse and, if his controller had his way, it would.

In the meantime, they had to keep moving. 'Come

on,' he said, and he looked around for a new route through the crawlspace.

'If it's about my running away,' Olvir began, but Kari cut him off.

'Forget that. It's them.' She looked over to where Nyssa and the Doctor were standing by the navigation screen, discussing the possible implications of the expanded star-chart. 'They can't be trusted. They teamed up and took my gun away.'

'You've got it back.'

'That's not the point. Stick with your own kind and tell them nothing else.'

'My own kind?' Olvir said with some incredulity. 'It's our own kind who cut loose and dumped us here. You'd do the same to me now, if you got the chance.'

'No, I wouldn't.'

Olvir looked at her suddenly, with searching interest and some hope. 'Really?' he said.

'Of course I wouldn't,' Kari said, trying not to appear as uncomfortable as she felt.

Olvir watched her a moment longer, and then shrugged. 'You'd say that anyway,' he said.

The star-chart on its own was of no use. Both the Doctor and Nyssa agreed that it was an interesting curiosity which told them nothing. It was a clue, not a solution, and they didn't even know the true nature of the problem. As far as the Doctor was concerned, this argued the need for the analytical resources of the lost TARDIS. Nyssa was worried about the prospect of taking the danger of infection back to Tegan and Turlough, whom she assumed to be safe and waiting inside, but the Doctor believed that the danger had begun the moment that the door to the liner had

70

opened.

In the meantime, they were getting no closer. Olvir and Kari finished their conversation and came over. Kari said, 'Any progress?'

'Nothing,' the Doctor said, and he indicated the console with its scattering of useless memory blocks alongside. 'If there's a map of the liner, it isn't here.'

Olvir looked down for a moment, and then said, 'Why not try some of the others?'

The Doctor frowned. 'What others?'

Olvir indicated the equipment stacks where he'd been hiding. 'Those little blocks,' he said. 'There's a rack full of them back there.'

Bor had taken a walk.

Valgard had seen him go and had been able to do nothing about it. Once he'd passed the crude yellow line that marked the beginning of the forbidden zone, he was as good as lost. Valgard had called to him, but Bor had only hesitated briefly and shouted something that sounded like *It's still climbing*. His helmet was off and he was looking worse than ever, a ragged scarecrow of a man who was obviously unwell and feverish.

Valgard stood at the line in the middle of the storeyard and watched as Bor disappeared into the shadows that began on the far side of the area and stretched away into the depths of the Terminus. He wasn't the first to walk off into the zone, and he probably wouldn't be the last. For a moment Valgard saw another figure in place of Bor, and its face was his own.

Perhaps it wasn't too late. Perhaps something could be done before Bor was overpowered by the fast-

71

acting sickness that gave the forbidden zone its name, and he could be brought back ... back to suffer the slow, creeping deterioration that no amount of armour or drug control could fully prevent.

All of the Vanir were dead men – Bor, Valgard, Eirak, all of them. Perhaps a walk into the forbidden zone was the most that they could look forward to, release from the endless workload of Lazars that arrived in increasing numbers and went ... well, nobody really knew where they went. It was the Vanir's job to ensure that they got from the liners and into the Terminus. Once they'd been taken into the zone, that job ended.

For as long as it took these thoughts to go through his mind, Valgard hesitated. Letting Bor go the way of his choice might, in the end, be the kindest thing to do. Except that Valgard couldn't bring himself to do it. He went to speak to Eirak.

The watch-commander of the Vanir was to be found in the corner of a converted storage tank that he used as an administrative office. Here he would sit and puzzle over worksheets and shift allocations as he did his best to handle the inflow of Lazars with an ailing labour force. If the throughput was slowed, Lazars died on his hands; and Terminus Incorporated had its own way of punishing such inefficiency.

Eirak hadn't long returned from giving the sterilisation order to the current liner's drones – and at the same time, although he couldn't know it, he'd given Tegan one of the biggest scares of her life – when Valgard burst in.

'Eirak,' he said, even before he'd removed his radiation helmet in the comparative safety of the tank, 'We've got a problem.'

Eirak rubbed his eyes wearily. Without his helmet he was nothing like the monster that Tegan might have expected. He was simply a tired bureaucrat, and problems tended to form long queues for his attention.

'Really?' he said.

Valgard advanced on the desk, and set his helmet down with a thump. It partly covered the chart that Eirak had been studying, but Valgard didn't seem to notice. 'It's Bor. He just turned around and walked off the job. He went straight into the forbidden zone.'

'Why?'

'No reason. Nothing obvious, anyway.'

Eirak frowned. 'That's all we need,' he said, partway lifting Valgard's helmet and pulling the chart free. 'I'll have to revise the entire roster.'

Valgard waited for a moment, but Eirak was already reabsorbed in the graph. He couldn't stay silent for long. 'Is that all you're going to say?'

'I've got a shipload of Lazars just arrived, we're under-strength and most of the men are too sick to work more than a half-shift. What do you expect me to say?'

'There must be something you can do.'

Eirak sighed. 'Like what? Grow up, Valgard.'

Valgard took an angry step around the makeshift table. 'You've got a responsibility ...' he began, but Eirak suddenly thrust a handful of the papers before him, almost crumpling them before Valgard's eyes.

'*This* is my responsibility,' he snapped. 'To keep the Terminus running so that we all get some chance of staying alive. What Bor does is Bor's problem. The rosters and the work schedules are mine.'

'So you'll just let him go?'

Eirak's expression changed. The anger went, and the real Eirak was uncovered – the ruthless, calculating personality that had fitted him so well for his self-appointed job in the Terminus. He said, smooth as a snake and twice as dangerous, 'Do *you* want to bring him back? I could give you the order.'

For one moment, Valgard was revisited by the fleeting glimpse that he'd had in the storeyard, his own face looking back from the other side of the line. 'You couldn't make it stick,' he said.

'Oh, but I could.' Eirak's fingers drifted lightly over some of the papers on his desk, touching them, almost loving them. 'How long would you last without a food ration? Or Hydromel?'

Valgard was beaten, and he knew it. Eirak had the power to withold the symptom-suppressing drug simply because the others all knew how much they needed him. When Valgard said nothing, Eirak went on, 'Get Sigurd and check out the liner. And forget about Bor, he's taken the easy way out.'

Nothing happened.

Eirak met Valgard's eyes and repeated, with a steely edge, 'Check the liner.'

Valgard turned and walked out.

The fifth block that they tried carried maintenance details for the liner, and several of the diagrams were given over to breakdowns of the corridor systems on each deck. They weren't exactly a tourist map, but they would do.

'It looks complicated,' Nyssa said.

'Like a maze,' the Doctor agreed. 'No wonder we got lost.' He stared for a while, fixing the details into his memory. There was a certain pattern in the layout of the passageways, but it would have taken a long time to perceive it by wandering around. The diagram couldn't tell him where to find the TARDIS, but it would at least prevent them from wandering in circles as they looked for the link.

'We can put a bit more method into the search this way,' he explained when Kari asked him about the computer's usefulness. 'We can't afford to waste any time on uncertainties, now we know that there's disease around.' He was about to say more, but the lights went out.

'Everybody down!' Kari shouted, and such was her tone of command that everybody went. She whispered something else, and Olvir did a silent sprint across the control room to take up a position beside the door, burner at the ready.

As the Doctor's eyes slowly adjusted to the new light levels, he realised that the liner had simply returned itself to the state of readiness it had shown on their arrival. 'What's happening?' Nyssa wanted to know, and the Doctor nodded towards the control centre under the window. Before he could speak, the liner's automated voice was booming all around them.

'*Attention,*' it said. '*Preparations for departure will begin with stage-one sterilisation. Unprotected personnel are advised to leave this liner immediately. No return will be permitted.*'

'No one outside,' Olvir reported.

'*Terminus Incorporated will accept no responsibility for the consequences of ignoring this warning. Stage-one sterilisation is now commencing.*'

The Doctor and Nyssa exchanged an apprehensive look.

It was quite a relief for Tegan and Turlough to come into an area where they could at least stand, even though they had to hunch a little to avoid banging their heads. The service core, as Tegan had named it, was a metal cage with a walkway floor that appeared to run the full length of the ship. It was obviously intended to give access to various underfloor areas, and because of this it seemed likely that they'd soon come upon a more orthodox way out.

'Maybe we're safer down here,' Turlough said, remembering what they'd seen only a little while before, but Tegan was doing her best to put this out of her mind.

'Come on,' she said, and started off ahead. There was some light, but most of it came from bad shielding where there should have been none. Turlough was slow in following; when Tegan looked back, she saw him standing and inspecting the floor beneath him.

'What's the matter?' she said.

He seemed hesitant, but he stepped forward. 'I felt the floor move ...' he began, but before he could finish he was gone.

The walkway floor was no more than a series of thin alloy sections bolted to an underframe, and one of them had been loose. Tegan had stepped on its centre, but Turlough had put his weight too close to the edge – it had hinged under him as quickly and efficiently as the slickest trapdoor and dumped him through the resulting gap.

Tegan dashed to him. He was hanging onto the edge, his knuckles whitening as they fought for a grip where there was none. In the long darkness below him, the breakaway section was still falling. His hands slid a couple of inches and his legs kicked free in space, but then Tegan grabbed both of his wrists and held him firm.

There was a booming crash, far-off and echoing. Tegan pulled as hard as she could, but she was holding Turlough's weight almost unaided.

'Don't kick!' she said. 'You make it worse.'

Turlough did his best to be calm, even though his heart was racing. He tried to let himself swing free. Tegan hauled again, and they made a few inches – enough for him to get a fingerhold over the next join in the flooring. Now that he could help, Tegan reached over and grabbed a handful of his collar. She got a handful of his shoulder too, but he didn't complain. Slowly, his muscles singing like violin strings, Turlough came up and over the edge to safety.

They lay together, gasping. Tegan was still holding him, as if there was some danger that he might slide back. The only sound besides their ragged breathing was the howl of moving air in the vast space below.

But then it slowly became clear to Turlough that the added rumbling that he'd been taking for granted wasn't simply the blood pounding in his ears.

'What's that?' he said, wondering if it was the working of his imagination, but Tegan had also heard something.

'I don't know,' she said. 'I don't like it.'

They barely had time to duck before the high-pressure sterilising gas was on them.

Kari's suggestion for speeding up the search for the TARDIS – that they should split into two groups and keep in contact via the hand-radios – hadn't really found much favour with the Doctor, but with the new urgency that had been added to the situation he really had little choice. Nyssa insisted that she'd be safe with Olvir, and so the Doctor reluctantly agreed.

'See you at the TARDIS,' Nyssa said, before she and Olvir disappeared from sight.

Kari was about to set off in the opposite direction, but the Doctor held her back for a moment. 'We can't waste time,' she protested.

'I know,' the Doctor said, 'but there's something we have to understand before we go any further.'

'What?'

'It doesn't matter who finds the TARDIS first. But nobody gets left, dumped or abandoned. All right?'

Kari hesitated. She seemed almost evasive, and it was obvious that she was overcoming her most immediate response. 'Of course,' she said eventually.

Ah, well, the Doctor thought, *at least she's learning*. They moved out.

The search proceeded at speed, both parties moving in parallel around opposite sides of the liner. Olvir almost ran all the way, as if he felt he had something to prove, but the main consequence of this was that Nyssa found it harder and harder to keep up.

'I have to stop,' she said eventually.

'We can't,' Olvir told her. 'Come on.'

'Please …' She stumbled, and Olvir had to catch her. It was then that he realised that his haste could actually defeat the object of the search. 'I had a dose of temporal instability,' she explained trying to catch her breath. 'I've been feeling bad ever since.'

He helped her down to sit on the floor against the corridor wall. 'A minute,' he said, 'no more. I'll tell the others.' And then he crouched beside her and unclipped the radio from his belt.

As soon as he switched it on, he knew that any

attempt to communicate from this part of the ship would be pointless; the air was filled with a weakly pulsating interference from the radio's speaker.

'We've got a problem,' Nyssa said quietly.

'It's just leak interference,' Olvir assured her. 'Bad shielding on the engines somewhere.'

'That's not what I meant. Look.'

So Olvir looked, and got his first view of one of the liner's drones.

It stood squarely in the corridor before them, with the low-level lights glinting on the blades and drills by its sides. These were the only parts of the liner that Olvir had seen which didn't look shabby. It seemed to be waiting for something.

'There's no need for panic,' Olvir said, hoping that he sounded confident.

'I'm not panicking. I'm *ill*.'

'Can you stand up?'

'The problem is breathing.' Nyssa fumbled at her bodice in the shadows. Something ripped, and there was a clink of metal as something dropped to the floor.

'Don't make any sudden moves,' Olvir said. 'I don't like the look of those weapons.'

But Nyssa was starting to sound impatient with him. She couldn't fight the reason for her discomfort, and Olvir just happened to be the next in line. 'They're not weapons,' she said, 'they're tools. It's a maintenance robot. Anyone can see that.'

'So what's the problem?'

'They're sterilising the place, and we're in the way.'

Olvir thought it over. If the drone really was no threat, then all they'd need to do would be to get up and walk away. It hadn't moved.

79

'Let's go,' he said and, moving slowly, he helped Nyssa to her feet. He couldn't help noticing that she leaned on him heavily. She came up into the weak light of the corridor and turned her face towards him.

She'd grown paler. Her skin was almost white, and her lips had darkened. Olvir felt a terrible wrench inside as he realised where he'd seen such a face before. He released her, and stepped back in horror.

'Olvir,' she said, alarmed, 'what's wrong?'

But Olvir could only shake his head. He couldn't speak. As if it had now received the signal that it had been waiting for, the drone moved forward.

And as it moved, the control voice echoed again around the ship. '*Attention,*' it said. '*This is the final warning. All Lazars and any other personnel must disembark immediately ...*'

(The drone extended a three-fingered clamp towards Nyssa, reaching for her wrist.)

'*Stage-two sterilisation is about to begin. Drones will give assistance to those Lazars requiring it ...*'

(Gently, it began to draw her away from Olvir; he did nothing to prevent it.)

'*All other personnel must leave immediately ...*'

(Nyssa called for his help, but he could only stare as the voice continued.)

'*All Lazars must comply with the drones. All Lazars must comply with the drones. Stage-two sterilisation is about to begin.*'

Olvir stood alone in the corridor, though in his mind he was somewhere else. His father and his uncle were talking downstairs. Papers were being drawn up, some kind of loan was being agreed. His father and his mother were arguing. It was the hour before the dawn, and the sap-scent of the leaves in his uncle's

80

garden came to him on the dew-damp breeze. His uncle walked alone down the street, a crumpled piece of paper in his hand. Olvir's hands were sore from the digging. The earth was over his head, and still they dug deeper, the shovels biting into the hard clay almost all of the way down to bedrock. He stood back from the edge of the hole, and the sap-scent of the garden was burned away by the sour smell of the lime. The empty bags lay by the side of the grave, and his hands were blistered now as they shovelled dark earth back into the hole.

Olvir stood alone in the corridor. In his mind, he was somewhere else.

Valgard had done as he was told because he knew that, when it came down to it, Eirak's hold over the Vanir was unbreakable. He could grouse about it as he and Sigurd rode the freight elevator to the receiving platform against the liner's side, but he couldn't do anything.

Sigurd listened, but he wasn't over-sympathetic. 'And what did Eirak say?'

'He didn't want to know. He was more concerned about the effect on the rosters.'

There were a couple of Lazars waiting when the two Vanir reached the platform. They were standing blinded in the air-seal section that linked the Terminus to the liner, shivering and not making a sound. Valgard and Sigurd herded them into the elevator. Another Vanir work detail had already transferred most of the 'passengers' down into the main part of the Terminus, but the drones always managed to round up a few stragglers.

'Don't cross him, Valgard,' Sigurd warned as he

closed the cage door on the Lazars. He and Valgard remained on the platform as the elevator dropped away.

'He doesn't scare me,' Valgard said.

'He should. He's got too much power around here.'

'He's a glorified clerk, that's all. Anybody could do what he does.'

But Sigurd shook his head. 'One or two have tried, and it's not so easy. Without Eirak, the Terminus won't work.'

'That would be the company's problem,' Valgard said, but even to him it sounded hollow.

An indicator light over the elevator control came on; the cage had been emptied down below. Sigurd threw the switch for its return, and said, 'I'll tell you what the company would do. They'd starve us out and then find some other prison willing to sell off its hard cases as forced labour. Face it, Valgard, we just don't count.'

And the galling part about it was, as Valgard knew, that Sigurd was right. Terminus Incorporated had wanted a low-cost, trouble-free workforce, and they had it in the corps they called the Vanir. The rules were simple; work or die. And the means of control was the drug that they called Hydromel.

Valgard said, 'So Bor dies,' and Sigurd shrugged.

'We're all dying here anyway,' he said. 'Bor just took the easy way out.'

'That's what Eirak told me.'

'Well, he knows what he's talking about. Come on.'

It was time to check the liner, and to collect their consignment of Hydromel from the control room. It would be packed into a metal case that fitted into a slot in the automated unit by the windows. Any

82

attempt to remove it before the brief period between disembarkation and stage-two sterlisation, and the locks would go on. They moved towards the liner, but their way was blocked.

One of the drones had managed to come up with another Lazar. It was still gripping her wrist as she stood there, wide-eyed and scared. She looked almost alert, but Valgard knew how deceptive appearances could be. The best way to keep your sanity in the Terminus was to forget that these things had ever been human. Then when the company's radiation-resistant trained mule took them off into the zone, you were safe from any worries about what lay ahead of them.

Now time was getting short. Valgard said that he'd take care of the Lazar if Sigurd went in to get the Hydromel. Sigurd agreed, and as he disappeared through the air-seal Valgard half-dragged and half-carried the girl across to the returned elevator – there was no point in expecting a Lazar to understand you or manage for itself.

Inside the cage, Nyssa grabbed the bars to stop herself from falling. She felt as if she'd stumbled into somebody else's nightmare without knowing the aims of the plot or the story so far. Her new jailer entered after her and stood blocking the way out, but this seemed to be incidental – he obviously didn't expect her to run anywhere, and for Nyssa's part she couldn't immediately think of anywhere to run.

He was wearing dark armour and a cloak, but for the moment he'd removed his helmet. He seemed weary, a gaunt and haggard man with thinning hair that hung almost to his shoulders. Nyssa took a deep breath and said, 'Where are you taking me?'

Valgard looked at her sharply. 'They don't usually speak,' he said.

There was a coldness in him that Nyssa didn't find encouraging, but she pressed herself to go on. 'I'm not one of the Lazars.'

'You should see yourself. The drones are programmed to recognise the symptoms, anyway.'

It took Nyssa a long moment to absorb this. She'd had no illusions about the dangers of infection, but to learn that it had already happened to her ... It had arrived so fast. What kind of disease could it be? And why – this was a fleeting thought that she was later to wish that she'd given more attention – why didn't her new jailer seem worried by being so close to it?

She said, 'Are you doctors?'

'Doctors?' Valgard was bitterly amused. 'We're baggage-handlers. We just receive and pass on.'

'But I have to know what's happening to me.'

'You'll be given to the Garm,' Valgard told her in a tone which suggested she'd already used up more of his patience than she had a right to expect, 'and he'll take you into the forbidden zone. And that's the last that anybody here will see of you.' And then he half-turned away to watch the liner for Sigurd's reappearance.

Garm? Forbidden zone? Whatever lay ahead, it sounded grim. And her hand was starting to hurt. She held it up and saw a spot of blood lying as fat as a bead on her thumb. It must have happened as she'd tried to ease her breathing in the liner corridor. She'd felt the jab, but she only remembered it now.

Valgard was watching her out of the corner of his eye, and he was getting suspicious. He couldn't tell for sure whether or not she was trying to conceal something in her hand. He said, 'What are you doing?'

Nyssa turned to show him. 'I cut my thumb,' she said. 'Look.'

She put out her hand for Valgard to see, and he automatically leaned closer. It was then that she changed the gesture into a fast upward sweep with the heel of her hand that caught the Vanir on the point of the chin.

He staggered back, and Nyssa ran from the elevator. The platform outside was small, and there were only two choices: a metal runged stairway that she could see over to one side and which probably served for access if the elevator wasn't working, and the liner itself. Inside the liner were the Doctor and the TARDIS; it was really no choice at all.

In the doorway, she paused just long enough to take a look back. Valgard was emerging in pursuit, and he didn't look pleased. If she could keep her lead (and ignore the weakness that was already beginning to pull her down) she could perhaps lose him in the complex of internal passageways. She turned, and ran straight into Sigurd.

He caught her wrist easily, and held her fast. 'Come on,' he said. 'Valgard's not *that* ugly.'

Nyssa could only struggle weakly as she was taken into the elevator for the second time. Valgard was looking embarrassed, and Sigurd said, 'Are you getting old?'

'No, just gullible.' Valgard glanced at the familiar metal case in Sigurd's free hand. 'Did you check through all the levels?'

'You're joking. If there's anybody left, the drones can flush them out.'

The cage door was closed, the interior switch was thrown. There was a lurch, and they started to descend. Within a few metres, Nyssa was getting her first real view of the Terminus.

They were dropping through a complex of catwalks that ran all around the open shaft. Nyssa's immediate impressions were of darkness, bare metal, oil, and steam, but then the steam cleared and she was looking out into an immense interior space. It was like the inside of a gutted whale, or perhaps some bizarre parody of a cathedral under restoration. The best-lit areas were far below; elsewhere the lights were strung out and temporary-looking, and the presence of a large amount of what appeared to be scaffolding and tarpaulin sheeting only added to the makeshift effect. Behind these layers of evidence of human activity was the dark presence of the Terminus itself, over-powering all attempts to create brightness, and making them small.

Nyssa was glad of the bars to hold onto. Something out there was being prepared, just for her.

'We can't have missed it,' the Doctor said, perplexed and frustrated. They'd covered their own part of the liner and had no success at all. The same was presumably true of Olvir and Nyssa, since they hadn't radioed.

Kari said, 'How about the other explanation?'

'What?'

'It's disappeared.'

But the Doctor shook his head. 'There was a book lying on the floor,' he explained. He couldn't know that the biotechnical text from the TARDIS's library was at that moment being flash-burned in the liner's incinerator along with a bagful of beads and several kilos of discarded bandages, all collected in the drones' anti-litter campaign. 'It would still be...' The Doctor tailed off. In looking at the floor he'd seen something else, and he moved over to pick it up.

It was a piece of material, a part of Nyssa's skirt. In the bad light they'd almost missed it. 'There's blood,' the Doctor said. 'Call Olvir. Quickly.'

Nyssa's first impression – that the human activity in the Terminus was a recent overlay on some much older structure – was confirmed when they reached the lowest level. The large tunnel structures that ran through the middle of the ship were original, as were the massive fuel or liquid storage tanks that stood in rows on either side of these. The crudely cut doors which converted these tanks into rooms and the walkways that linked them, however, were obviously by some different hand. They'd been squeezed in wherever they'd fit, and the standard of workmanship was low.

Some of the tanks appeared to have been put to use as holding wards for the Lazars. Nyssa could see a few of the sick people, hardly more than bundles of bone and rag, waiting to be moved inside by the Vanir. The workforce showed no cruelty, but no tenderness, either. Valgard's description of them as baggage-handlers seemed to be as apt as any. They prodded and pushed where they had to, using their metal staffs as shepherds might. The Lazars, for their part, obeyed like sheep.

And I'm one of them, Nyssa thought. The thought didn't scare her as much as it should. She knew that it would get worse when the realisation hit her for sure.

Eirak watched the two Vanir unloading the girl.
Like all the others, he wore full armour for maximum
protection out in the open areas of the Terminus.
When he moved towards Sigurd with his hand
outstretched, there was no question about what he
wanted. Sigurd handed over the Hydromel case.

Eirak hefted it expertly, testing its weight against
his memory of countless earlier consignments.

'It's light,' he said.

Sigurd was taken aback. 'They can't cut us down
again,' he said.

'This stuff's expensive. They won't send us any
more than the minimum.'

'We could all die, and they wouldn't even know it,'
Sigurd said bitterly.

'They'd know it,' Eirak assured him. 'They've got
ways of knowing. Has anyone warned the Garm about
Bor?'

This last question was mainly aimed at Valgard, but
he stood with a tight grip on the arm of the last girl out
of the shuttle and seemed to be making a point of
ignoring his watch-commander. Sigurd said, 'I don't
know. Why?'

'We'll need the body back for the armour.
Valgard!'

So now Valgard couldn't help but turn and listen.
Eirak went on, 'It's your job. Sigurd can see to the
girl.'

Valgard reluctantly released his grip, and Sigurd
took over. 'It's just as well,' he said to Valgard in a
lowered voice that wasn't entirely serious. 'She might
take another crack at you.'

But it was impossible to make any kind of a private
remark, not with helmet amplifications. 'What does

that mean?' Eirak said sharply.

'Nothing,' Sigurd said, but the damage was done.

Eirak was needling him, Valgard was sure of it. He already had other duties, as Eirak well knew – after all, he'd been the one who had assigned them. Now in addition he had to go back to the storeyard, the very place where he'd seen Bor walk off into the zone, and there he had to call the Garm.

The storeyard was exactly what its name implied, an area where the leftovers and spare units of the builders'-yard junk that cluttered the Terminus had been heaped. It had been set up by whoever had carried out the conversion a long time before. In those days the boundary to the zone had been a lot further away, but it had since been redefined to run straight across the middle of the yard's open area. It was to this spot that they brought the Lazars when it was time for them to be taken into the zone. Nobody visited the place otherwise – from the radiation point of view it was too 'hot' to be comfortable for long – unless it was to perform a periodic check on the zone monitoring gear, as he and Bor had been doing, or to call the Garm.

There was a switchbox bolted to one of the girder uprights near the edge of the zone. Valgard passed his hand before the sensor plate and felt the gut-trembling hum of the subsonic signal as it went out. The Garm would be with him soon. It didn't have a choice.

The Garm was Terminus Incorporated's answer to the difficulties of deploying any kind of workforce in the zone. It wasn't that they had any moral hesitation over the matter. If the company thought that it could make the system pay, the Vanir would be ordered in and some strategy would be devised to force them to obey. But the fact was that it would be uneconomical: working just outside the hottest areas with their symptoms held in check by drug control, they could last for years; inside the zone they'd be dead within days.

It was for this reason that the Garm had been brought in. It was an animal from some planet where the background levels of radiation were naturally high, no doubt from some suicidal war somewhere in its past. The Garm was already adapted to zone-like conditions, and Terminus Incorporated technicians had gone in with their conditioning techniques and a spot of supporting surgery in order to get maximum compliance and obedience out of it.

It was a while before Valgard realised that he wasn't alone. For all its size, the Garm moved in silence. And it kept to the shadows – even now Valgard could only just make out its massive dog-headed outline and the dull red gleam of its eyes in the darkness.

'Garm!' he said. 'Can you hear me?'

The Garm inclined its head slightly.

'One of the Vanir's gone missing. He walked across into the zone. When you find his body you're to bring it back here, you understand?'

Again, the slight movement of assent.

Valgard lowered his voice a little. 'Apart from that, we've got more Lazars for you to move. Big surprise, eh?'

The Garm showed no response. Back in the early days they'd argued over whether the Garm had any intelligence or not, but the consensus had been that anything working in the zone without complaint and

90

for no reward would even make Skeri look bright. Skeri had been the first of the Vanir to take his own life. Looking back, perhaps he hadn't been so dumb.

Well, Valgard had a job to do. He turned and walked away.

Intelligent or not, there was something in the Garm's presence that had always made him uneasy. He was glad to leave.

'There,' the Doctor said, pointing, 'another drop of blood.'

Kari couldn't understand it. Nyssa had left an inadvertent trail – and recently, too, from the look of it – that diverged wildly from the pattern that had been laid down. Now they were being led down the stairs to the next deck of the liner. 'But why here?' she said. It didn't make any sense.

'Try them again,' the Doctor urged. Kari's first attempt with the radio had produced no response. She raised the handset and switched it on, but frowned at the pulsating interference she heard.

'There must be a radiation leak somewhere around here,' she said. 'It'll clear if we move.' She was about to switch off, but the Doctor seemed interested. He held out his hand for the radio, and she gave it to him. He waved it back and forth, using the interference as a crude means of detection.

'That's the wave pattern the TARDIS homed in on,' the Doctor said. 'But it's weak ...'

'Can't that wait?' Kari said, and the intuitive leap that the Doctor had been on the point of making had to be postponed.

'Yes, of course,' he said, and bent again to check the direction of the trail. Downward and outward – it was starting to seem as if Nyssa had been making purposefully for the exit as it had been shown in the computer layout.

Some distance away, Tegan and Turlough were straining to listen.

'It's him,' Tegan said, 'I'm sure of it.'

Turlough frowned. The freak echo was too distorted for him to be sure. Misleading voices and wrong identification had already drawn them into one mess.

They had escaped the full effects of stage-one sterilisation by the coincidence of two near-disasters. High-pressure fumigating gas had been pumped through the below-decks areas without warning, a choking yellow cloud that threatened to poison them if they breathed it and suffocate them if they didn't. They'd been saved by the presence of a vent which funnelled the gas away instead of letting it stay around as a poison cloud. The vent was the hole through which Turlough had come close to falling.

Now they'd found an exit from the service core, but they were really no better off. They'd simply exchanged the crawlspaces for the ventilation system. As a means of getting around it ranked about equal; as a means of transmitting and distorting sound, it was full of surprises.

Back on the lower deck, the Doctor had stopped speaking. Kari looked at him to find out why, and then after a moment turned to see what had caught his attention.

Fog was boiling out of a side-corridor and spreading towards them.

'What is it?' she said.

'Stage-two sterilisation,' The Doctor told her. 'Come on.'

They backed off with haste. Elsewhere in the liner Tegan and Turlough were yelling in an attempt to get their attention, but it was too late. The heavy gas deadened any space that it filled, and now it seemed to be coming from every direction. With no handy vents and no alternative air supply, the Doctor knew that their chances of riding out the sterilisation were, as the automated voice had put it, small.

They were more than half-way to the exit, as the Doctor remembered it. Not an attractive course to take – but then they didn't have many options to choose from.

The door to the outside was dropping as they reached it, eyes streaming and gasping for breath. Kari would have done better if she'd kept a hold on her pressure helmet, but both she and Olvir had left them in the control room. They were a liability in combat, and they'd seemed unlikely to be necessary for a trip in the TARDIS.

They ducked under the falling edge of the door and emerged onto the receiving platform. Kari was already ahead, her burner raised and at the ready.

'I'm used to this,' she said, suddenly business-like and unarguably in command. 'Stay with me.'

The Doctor wasn't going to object. Kari had been trained in making sudden entries to strange and probably hostile situations, and such an advantage wasn't to be wasted. He said, 'What do we do?'

'First, we get to cover.'

No disputes so far. The receiving platform was as brightly lit as a boxing ring. The elevator shaft was empty and there was only one way to go, down the iron stairs to the side.

Even as they moved, the lights went out.

The Doctor was going to wait until his eyes adjusted, but Kari had a hold on his elbow and was pulling him along. He groped blindly for the guiderail, found it, and began to follow her down. They took it slowly, being careful to make as little noise as they could.

Within a minute, he could see. There was a dim glow around them, no more than a starlight overspill from the brighter areas somewhere down below, but it was enough. They were on part of a complex of catwalks that centred on the elevator shaft. Some ran along girders bolted between uprights, others were cable-suspended over long drops through darkness. Where two walks crossed over, a ladder or stairway would connect them. The entire structure appeared makeshift and frail.

Kari studied the way ahead. She was aware of the lit areas down below, and she wanted to pick a route which would avoid them. The object was not to seek confrontation, but to find somewhere away from danger so that they could discuss and decide their next move.

As she was evaluating, the Doctor was marvelling.

He'd moved to the catwalk rail and was looking down on the same scene that had appeared to Nyssa: the vast interior of the Terminus, and the antlike activity under the bright lights in a small section of it. 'Dante would have loved this,' he breathed – a living hell, complete with armoured dark angels.

'Reconnaissance comes later,' Kari said, and she pulled him away.

From his place by the lighting switches three levels below, Valgard watched them go in amazement. Outsiders? In the *Terminus*?

The area that Kari found for them seemed to be some kind of storeyard. It was on the 'ground-floor' level of the Terminus, but it was away from the occupied areas and further screened by a number of hung tarpaulins over a frame of scaffolding.

'The liner's no good to us now,' Kari said decisively. 'We'll have to find another way out.'

'You're combat section,' the Doctor reminded her. 'Leave the strategy to me.'

'But what's the alternative?'

'We've got Olvir and Nyssa to think about. Nyssa may be hurt – you saw the blood on the floor. I've got friends back in the TARDIS and they're trapped as surely as we are.'

'But we can't go back,' Kari pointed out.

'No,' the Doctor agreed, 'We can't. But in the end, we may have found that we had to come out into the Terminus anyway.'

'But why?'

'There's not only escape to think about. We take the risk of Lazar infection with us. And if there's an answer for that, I think we've a chance of finding it here.'

The Doctor pulled back a canvas cover. Underneath it was a stack of highly polished metal sheets standing on end. He looked at the distorted reflection of his own face. Nothing of the Lazar disease showing there ... but for how long?

Kari said, 'You think there's a cure for the disease?'

For a moment, the Doctor said nothing. He moved on through the storeyard. Finally he said, 'I think there's more to the Terminus than just an old dead ship.' Now he stopped before some kind of signal box that had been bolted to an upright. 'Didn't your chief think that there was anything strange about its position on the charts?'

Kari didn't answer. The Doctor let her chew on the idea for a while before he turned for her reactions.

Kari hadn't spoken, not because she was lost for a response but because a metal staff clamped crosswise on her neck was cutting off her air. Valgard had managed the hold in such a way that she could neither cry out nor reach her burner. Almost as the Doctor saw them, he released her. She slid to the floor in a graceless heap.

And then Valgard came for the Doctor.

The armoured Fury with its mailed hands outstretched, no part of the human being visible, would have been enough in itself to overcome opposition in many, and even the Doctor, who had seen more than his share of strange sights and weird aggressors, hesitated for a moment before he could react.

It was long enough. Valgard's hands clamped around his throat and started to squeeze.

Until now the Doctor hadn't been certain as to whether Valgard was a man or an artefact, but the pressure behind the gloved fingers was human. It was a limited kind of relief – hydraulically powered pincers would have decapitated him as easily as one might snip the head off a flower. The Doctor grabbed at Valgard's arms and tried to relieve the pressure, but Valgard responded by bearing down more heavily.

They struggled in silence. The Doctor wasn't having much success. Everything started to turn grey, and then red; and as blackness started to creep in from the edges of his vision, the Doctor knew that the situation was becoming desperate.

He could see, dimly and far away, that Kari was stirring. Her speed of reaction was a tribute to her training. Within a few seconds she was fully alert and reaching for her burner.

Some sign of hope must have shown in the Doctor's eyes. Valgard swung him around. The pressure eased for a moment, and then the Doctor was shielding the Vanir from Kari's weapon. There was no way that she could get a clear shot.

She fired.

The burner spat a continuous red beam. She'd opened it up to full intensity. She was aiming wide of the mark, and the Doctor could immediately see what her intentions were. Valgard couldn't ... but then, that was the idea.

Kari was aiming at the reflective sheet that the Doctor had uncovered only a couple of minutes before. A couple of minutes? It seemed like hours ... but then the Doctor realised that he was losing his hold on consciousness, and he fought to get his mind back in focus. The energy beam was being reflected from the sheet at an angle which took it only a metre or so behind Valgard's all-enclosing helmet.

The less-than-perfect reflectivity of the surface meant that the beam was starting to get diffuse as it came close, but it would have to do. The Doctor pretended to weaken suddenly, and Valgard was so taken by surprise that he almost overbalanced. He was even more surprised when his victim came surging back with renewed strength, enough to force him back a pace. And then another.

Valgard's helmet passed directly through the path of the beam. There was a searing flash and a sound like lightning in water, and suddenly it was all over. Valgard clutched at his head and fell with a crash.

The Doctor felt as if he'd been the tester in a noose-tying contest. Any more, and he was sure that he'd have been carrying his own head around in a bowling-ball bag. Valgard was making weak struggling motions, trying to get his helmet off. He was down, but he certainly wasn't out.

Kari came over and stood by the Doctor. She took the back-up power pack from her belt and plugged it into the burner. That one long burst of energy had drained it completely. She said, 'Is it a machine?'

'It's a man.' Speaking was like spitting glass, but it didn't feel as if there had been any permanent damage. The Doctor went on, 'He's wearing radiation armour. Keep him covered.'

Valgard was already making the effort to sit up. Kari said, 'There's a problem.' She said it in the quiet, unexcited way that people save for the worst disasters.

'What do you mean?'

'The back-up unit's dead. I've no power.'

Valgard had made it to his knees, and they had no way of stopping him.

'Come on then,' the Doctor said. When it came to a choice between fighting and running, the Doctor preferred to run every time. Those who stayed to fight tended to be swiftly stripped of their noble illusions. They took aim for the darkness, and ran.

Valgard struggled a little longer, and finally managed to remove his helmet. It had protected him from the worst of the blast, but the heat had sealed all of its ventilation lines and crazed the one-way glass of the visor. He'd been blind and baking inside – the useless piece of armour was trailing steam as he let it fall to the floor. Flushed and panting, he looked around. The intruders were gone, but the sound of their running footsteps echoed back to him.

He'd followed as far as he could, and he could follow no further. They'd gone straight into the zone.

'Anybody coming after us?' the Doctor said when they stopped for breath.

Kari checked behind them. 'No.'

'Let me have your radio.'

She handed it over without question. Now, more than ever, they needed to get a warning to the others – wherever they were. But she'd misunderstood the Doctor's intention. She kept watch for pursuers, saying, 'If they wear radiation armour, there must be radiation.'

'That's what I'm checking,' the Doctor said, and he held the radio out at arm's length and switched it on.

A pulsating waveform came through, strong and loud. It was similar to the interference they'd first heard on the liner, but it implied a much more serious leak. Kari said, 'Badly shielded engines again. Always the same pattern.'

The Doctor switched off the radio. They could forget about using it to communicate. There were properties of interference here that he'd never encountered before. He said, 'What kind of engines are they?'

'A self-containment reaction drive. It's like building a big bomb and then using the blast energy to form a container. Then you can skim off power whenever you need it.'

'No need of fuel, and it runs forever. What happens if anybody plugs the leaks?'

'You don't wait around to find out.'

The Doctor handed the set back to her. 'Let's move, then,' he said, and started out. Kari hesitated momentarily before she followed. She'd always believed that she could sense when she was being observed, and it had saved her in a couple of tight situations in the past. Now it seemed to be playing her false; there was a definite tingle, even though the more she looked the more certain she was that they were alone in the depths of the Terminus.

She put it out of her mind. That dull red gleam could have been anything.

The tank that Nyssa had come to think of as the Lazars' ward was bare, not too clean, and very poorly lit. Nyssa, like most of the others, sat on the floor by one of the walls. The worst cases were lying at the far end of the tank, in rough bunks, stacked like shelves from floor to ceiling.

She tried to use the time to do some coherent thinking about her position and the courses of action that were open to her, but concentration wouldn't come. It was like trying to catch hold of a spot of light on a wall.

So when two of the Vanir entered the tank and began checking the Lazars one by one, Nyssa was starting to get desperate. They'd left their helmets by the door (why did they seem so unafraid of infection?) and she recognised one of them from the receiving platform. When they got near enough, she'd speak to them.

This was Sigurd's least favourite part of the whole

operation, lifting heads and looking into one pair of dead eyes after another. As they moved along the lines he reported symptoms and made estimates on the chances of each Lazar making it as far as the zone. Some of them wouldn't even leave the tank alive. The other Vanir dutifully noted everything on a clipboard.

'I want to speak to somebody in charge,' one of them said suddenly as they came level. If Sigurd recognised Nyssa, he didn't show it.

'Speech centres untouched,' he dictated, ' could be a remissive.' The other Vanir made a note.

'Please listen,' Nyssa said, and reached out for his arm.

Sigurd caught her hand and tested its flexibility. 'General weakness,' he said, 'poor grip. But make a special note for Eirak.'

He straightened up, and the two Vanir moved on. Nyssa sank back, weak and defeated.

'You'll get nothing out of them,' the Lazar next to her whispered. 'They're not interested.'

Nyssa looked around in surprise. She'd come to believe that none of the Lazars was capable of speech, but the one alongside her was lifting back with difficulty the cloth that covered its head. This revealed a girl, a pale blonde of about Nyssa's age. She wasn't as far gone as any of the others, but the disease was surely squeezing the life and strength out of her.

'The only thing they care about,' she said, keeping her voice low so the Vanir wouldn't hear, 'is the drug that keeps them alive.'

'What are they going to do with us?'

'There's supposed to be a secret cure. But I think they're going to let us die.'

Nyssa was about to speak, but the girl stopped her. A moment later, the two Vanir walked by. They collected their helmets and left the tank. The door closed behind them with the solid clunk of metal on metal.

Nyssa said, 'One of them told me he was just a baggage-handler.'

The girl nodded. 'And we're the baggage.'

Nyssa summoned up her strength and tottered over to the door. She was amazed that her energy was seeping away so rapidly. The door operated on a simple key, but that was enough to ensure that she couldn't get out. She returned to her place.

'Might as well face it,' the girl said.

'No,' Nyssa said with determination.

'We've been had. There's no hospital and there's no cure. It's hopeless.'

'That's not what the Doctor would say.'

'There are no doctors here.'

'He's one of a kind. What's the forbidden zone?'

The girl said, with grudging admiration, 'You don't give up, do you?'

'Not until I'm beaten. Well?'

'I only know what I've heard. It's where the radiation gets too strong for them. They have to keep on this side of the line or they'll die even sooner.'

'And what's the Garm?'

'You'll find out soon enough.'

'I need to know now.'

The girl sighed. Talking was wearing her out, and she obviously believed that Nyssa's determination was going to be wasted. She said, 'It's some kind of animal they brought in to work in the zone. They operated on its brain, but it's still half wild.' She

102

turned to Nyssa, as much as she was able, and gave her a hard look.

'Just wait a little while longer,' she said, 'and you'll see for yourself.'

Sigurd came upon Eirak in his corner of the tank that was the Vanir's headquarters. The watch-commander was at his desk with the Hydromel case open before him, and he was making notes. Logging-in of the phials of honey-coloured liquid was always a priority duty.

Sigurd dropped his clipboard on the end of the desk, and said, 'Lazar assessment from tank three. How's it going?'

Eirak looked up at him. He wasn't smiling. He said, 'I was right. They've reduced the supply. Half of these are just coloured water.'

For a moment, Sigurd didn't know what to say. Finally he managed a strangled, 'But why?'

'Obviously they think we can get by on less. Or else we've not been performing well enough.'

'That's impossible.'

Eirak leaned back wearily, contemplating the glassware before him. 'I don't know how they get their information. Spies, perhaps.'

'Bor's gone,' Sigurd said with sudden inspiration. 'Won't that help?'

'Not enough. We'd have to lose at least one more.'

'Then there's no way out of it.'

'I just told you the way out,' Eirak said with quiet seriousness.

And he meant every word of it, Sigurd thought with horror. He's actually contemplating shutting one of us out. A name struck from a roster somehow didn't seem to carry the same charge of outrage as the death of a human being – but it was the rosters that were Eirak's reality. Sigurd was trying to think if he'd ever given Eirak a reason to single him out, but he could think of nothing that didn't apply to every other Vanir in the Terminus. Eirak won all the arguments, but still everybody griped. So it was really a question of who had offended him most recently.

As if in answer, Valgard burst into the tank.

'We've got trouble,' he said immediately. He was helmetless and in an obviously agitated state. The rest of the off-duty Vanir took an instant interest and started to come through from the bunkroom area.

Eirak looked up at him. 'What do you mean?' he said.

Valgard pushed his way through the growing crowd and leaned heavily on Eirak's desk. 'I saw two people down in the storeyard, a man and a girl. They went off into the zone.'

'Were they Lazars?'

Valgard shook his head. 'No, they weren't. They were talking about reconnaissance, and they were armed.'

'Company spies?' Sigurd hazarded.

'Perhaps.' Eirak obviously wasn't going to commit himself until he'd heard it all. He said to Valgard, 'Why didn't you stop them?'

'I tried, but they teamed up on me.'

'That's got to be it,' Sigurd insisted. 'The company sent them.'

But Eirak was still keeping his reserve. 'For what reason?'

'It's obvious,' Sigurd said. 'We've been here too long, and we've absorbed too much of the background radiation. Look what it did to Bor. They don't think we're giving them full value anymore. Unless we do something about it, we'll be making way for a new workforce. One that can do the job better.'

There was a general murmur of concern. Valgard wasn't convinced that they could act to help themselves. He said, 'But they're in the zone.'

'So we need a brave volunteer.' Eirak said, and he stared directly at Valgard. 'Don't we?'

There was a silence as realisation came to Valgard. Although he already knew the reason, he said quietly, 'Why me?'

'Because I know you'll succeed.'

'This isn't fair,' Sigurd started to say, but Eirak raised a hand to silence him.

The watch-commander's eyes didn't leave Valgard. 'Fairness doesn't come into it,' he said. 'There isn't enough Hydromel to go around, so I'm making a little bet with Valgard.' He reached out and closed the Hydromel case, twisting the small key in its lock. He'd already added a chain with a trembler alarm to ensure that no one would be able to interfere with the supply whilst it was unattended. He went on, 'He's had his last shot. But if he can put right his mistakes, he can have my supply.'

Valgard stared at him stonily. Then, without another word, he turned and walked out.

There was an overpowering feeling of relief in the tank. The Vanir broke up into a number of excitedly chattering groups. Only Sigurd stayed by Eirak.

'He'll die,' he protested, but Eirak was unruffled. In fact, he seemed pleased with himself.

'He hates me,' he said. 'He'll succeed.'

'And you'll give him your own Hydromel?'

Eirak gave him a pained look, one that said *how could you be so naive?*

It was no more nor less than Sigurd expected.

'Come on,' Eirak said loudly as he stood and reached for all the boards with the Lazar assessment forms, 'we've got Lazars to move.'

They were out.

After spending so long in the dark spaces of the liner that it seemed as if they'd take residence, Tegan and Turlough had managed to make their way into the duct system that fed air directly into the corridors. Turlough improvised a crowbar from a metal strut and used it to pry loose one of the covering grilles, and then completed the job by kicking it out two-footed. They crawled out into the corridor, grimy and streaked.

The TARDIS had faded away. Barring some fluke, the Doctor and Nyssa were either dead – which Turlough suggested but which Tegan wouldn't accept – or else they'd been forced outside by the sterilisation process. With this in mind, Tegan wanted to find the liner's control room. Perhaps there would be some way of opening the outside door from there.

They'd formed some idea of the liner's structure from their tour inside the walls, but it was still going to be a fairly haphazard search. It was further complicated by the fact that this seemed to be the time set aside for the drones to carry out their heavy maintenance work.

They crouched by a corner and listened to the sounds of welding, just out of sight. Occasional flashes threw long shadows across the intersection.

Tegan said, 'If they're programmed to get rid of

intruders, I don't want to find out the hard way. Did you see some of the knives they're carrying?'

'Weapons all around us,' Turlough said despondently. Tegan, of course, couldn't know what he meant.

'I suppose there are,' she said. 'Shall we move?'

They crept back until they felt it was safe, and then they started to walk. 'Tegan,' Turlough started to say, but he seemed uncertain how to go on.

'What?'

'Thanks for saving me.' It came out all at once.

Tegan was nonplussed. Gratitude was so against Turlough's nature – his *true* nature, as opposed to the polished and calculated exterior that he usually presented – that it had taken him a long time to get around to it. Which made her even more convinced that he was being sincere. Perhaps there was hope for him, after all.

'Don't mention it,' she said, and they moved on.

After a while, they took a break. Neither of them had realised how near to exhaustion they were getting. They sat on the steps of one of the inner-deck stairways, and Turlough said, 'You really think they made it to the outside?'

Tegan was hugging one of the stair rails and looking into nowhere. 'I know they're not dead,' she said.

'How?'

'I just know.'

There was a pause. Then: 'Tegan …'

'What?'

'If ever you had to kill someone, could you do it?'

She looked at him, frowning. 'What do you mean?'

'Just supposing. Could you?'

'No … I don't know. I suppose if it was important,

to save a friend or defend myself.'

'But if it was in cold blood?'

Tegan took hold of the rail and pulled herself to her feet. 'You're weird, Turlough,' she said. 'What a subject to bring up at a time like this.' And she started to ascend.

'We're just going deeper and deeper,' Kari complained. 'What are we looking for?'

'Whatever it is that makes the Terminus special,' the Doctor told her. 'Something that could even cure the Lazar disease.'

They'd really had little choice over their route. The ribbed tunnel that they'd entered hadn't offered them any interesting-looking diversions, and there seemed little point in returning when they knew that a hostile reception was guaranteed. Kari said, 'There's nothing here but radiation.'

The Doctor considered this for a moment. 'You know,' he said, 'you're right.' And he switched on the hand-radio for a brief burst of the wave interference. It was much louder than before. 'And we're getting closer to the source.'

'That doesn't sound too healthy.'

'It isn't. How safe is an engine when it leaks that badly?'

'You couldn't use it. You'd blow yourself away as soon as you tried to open up.'

'So,' the Doctor said, letting his mind run along the speculative rails that events had presented to it, 'why haven't they just dumped the reaction mass and made the Terminus radiation-free?'

'You think radiation's part of a cure?'

'I think there's even more to it than that,' the

Doctor told her. What Kari had suggested seemed, from the evidence, to be reasonable. If the Lazar disease was caused by a virus or a similar organism with a lower radiation tolerance, a non-lethal dose might be enough to clean it out of the victim's system. Blanket secrecy and social shame would serve to keep this simple solution from becoming common knowledge. Whoever ran the Terminus – the 'Terminus Incorporated' referred to in the liner's automated announcements – was obviously taking advantage of the old ship's high incidental levels without either knowing or caring how they were caused.

And the possible causes were beginning to worry the Doctor even more than the disease itself. 'We're standing at the centre of the known universe,' he told Kari. 'Now, don't you think that deserves some close consideration?'

But Kari was no longer listening to him. She seemed incredulous.

'I can hear someone *singing!*' she said.

Handling of the Lazars was conducted according to a plan originally devised by Eirak. Vanir responsibility for the sufferers technically ended at the yellow line when they were handed over to the Garm, but it seemed that the Company's judgement of their success was based on the survival rate as it was calculated somewhere later in the processing. What happened beyond the line was something that they couldn't know, but it was in their own interests to ensure that as many Lazars as possible arrived to face it alive.

Originally this had meant sending the sickest and least able through first. It looked good in theory, but in practice it was a disaster. They slowed up the whole process so much that even those who'd arrived able to walk on their own finally had to be carried to the handover point. Eirak's answer to this had been the Lazar assessment, where estimates of the advancement of the disease were made and the fittest sped through first. Which was how he came to be looking at Nyssa.

'She's hardly touched,' he said, putting a hand under her chin and tilting her face towards him.

'Well, compared to some of these,' Sigurd agreed. Other Vanir were moving amongst the Lazars and pinning numbered labels to them. It was all running in an orderly manner, the way that Eirak liked it.

'Take her first, then,' he said, straightening, and Sigurd turned to beckon one of the others over.

'No, wait,' Nyssa said quickly, and Eirak gave her the cool look that he saved for troublemakers. He'd been right, she was hardly touched. The progress of the disease barely seemed to have advanced beyond the initial stages.

He warned her, 'Don't give us a hard time.'

'But others are worse than me.'

'The fittest ones go first,' Eirak said. 'There's some kind of quota going, and most of these corpses won't fill it. So just co-operate and don't mess up our chances.'

He nodded to Sigurd. Two of the Vanir took Nyssa's arms and raised her, protesting, to her feet.

Tegan and Turlough had found the control room. They stood in the doorway, taking their first look.

'Maybe they were here,' Turlough said, but he didn't sound as if he believed it. Tegan was looking at

110

the two pressure helmets that had been abandoned on the main console.

'Maybe somebody was,' she said.

They moved in to look around. It wasn't as promising as Tegan had hoped. It was one thing to suppose that you'd be able to spot the control that you needed out of all the others, but facing the reality was something else. She wouldn't even know where to start.

Turlough reached over and tried a couple of switches. 'Hey,' Tegan said apprehensively, 'What are you doing?'

'Messing around, unless you've got a better idea.'

'Well, don't. The situation's bad enough.'

'We've got to try things,' Turlough insisted, and to demonstrate he tried a couple more. All of the screens at every crew position suddenly came alight. 'We can't just stand around. What if one of these opens the door to the outside?'

Tegan looked at the nearest screen. It showed a diagram which she couldn't understand, but which reminded her of the old-time maps which showed the earth at the centre of the universe, long before the spiral-arm backwater that was its true home had ever been imagined. She said, 'Do you think it could?'

'Well, how will we know if we don't try?'

Tegan came around the desk for a closer look.

Kari had been right. Somebody was singing to himself – breathlessly, tunelessly, and without much regard for the words. The song was something about being across the purple sea in the cold ground and sleeping peacefully, and the whole endless ramble was basically the same verse over and over with lines skipped, mumbled or hummed. When they came to the end of their tunnel, a cautious peek gave them a view of the singer.

'Who's that?' Kari said.

'He seems happy enough,' the Doctor said. 'Let's find out.'

He was hunched over and limping, obviously very ill. Part of his face, chest and arm had been blackened by an explosion that had ripped open his armour – the same kind of armour worn by their attacker only a short time before. There was a strap around his neck which had been knotted to make a sling for his twisted arm, but despite his injuries there seemed to be an odd cheerfulness about him, self-absorbed and purposeful.

His cloak was spread out on the floor behind him. There were three or four machine parts heaped on it. The hood was wrapped around his good hand, and he was dragging the haul onward into the Terminus. It seemed to be a painfully slow business. As they watched, he stumbled and fell to his knees.

The Doctor started to move out of cover, but Kari held him back.

'He's ill,' the Doctor said, and pulled free.

He cautiously approached the man, who was now making a weak effort to get up. Kari emerged from hiding, but she stayed some distance away.

The Doctor said, 'Can I help you?'

The man looked up. He didn't seem surprised. 'Most kind,' he said. 'A burden shared is a burden ... something or other.' And then he handed a part of his cloak to the Doctor, and made it up alone. The Doctor found that he was now expected to join in dragging the machine parts along. The man started

112

singing again.

The Doctor said, 'This isn't really what I had in mind.'

The man broke off his song. 'Oh?'

'I thought you were ill.'

'Ill?' He looked around in case the Doctor might be talking about someone else, but then he shook his head. 'No,' he said, and resumed his dragging.

The Doctor looked back over his shoulder. Kari was, if her expression was anything to go by, getting pretty exasperated. He beckoned for her to follow.

The load was heavy even with two of them pulling, and after a short time the man called a halt. He lowered himself to sit on the floor, exhausted.

'Many thanks,' he said. 'Aid much appreciated. Just a short breather before the, ah, final ... whatever ...'

'Any time,' the Doctor told him. Now it was time to face Kari. She was looking angry.

'You're breaking every rule in the book,' she said.

'Then we work by different books.'

She held up her useless burner. 'You could have been walking right into danger, and I couldn't have helped you.'

'He's harmless. Which is more than I can say for the rest of the wildlife that we've encountered in the Terminus.'

'And what do you think he can do for us?'

'With careful handling, we can get him to explain the set-up here,' the Doctor began, but it was at this point they realised they were again alone. There was only one way that the cabaret could have gone, and the Doctor and Kari moved as one to follow him.

They were expecting to find a further extension of

the tunnels, instead they found where the tunnels led: to the engines of the Terminus ship.

They were held in spherical reactor globes, supported in steel cradles with coolant pipes and control cables snaking around, and each had a tiny inspection window. The glass would be leaded and tinted to near-opacity, but so fierce were the energies inside that each glowed like a tiny sun – that is, with the exception of the globe immediately to their left. This globe was dark and dead-looking.

The man had made it all the way to the far end of the row. This obviously wasn't his first visit, because there was a heap of junk, scrap and odd machine parts stacked in front of the globe. Now, ineffectually shielding his face with his arm, he was trying to lift a piece from his latest haul and place it on top.

'There's our radiation source,' the Doctor said.

Kari didn't understand. 'A junkheap?'

'The globe. It's cracked.'

The man managed to add to the pile, but he fell back after the effort. The Doctor and Kari caught him, one on each side. 'Easy now,' the Doctor said, and they guided him to a safe distance and sat him against the support structure of the inactive globe.

'Most kind,' he said. 'I ...' he hesitated, and squinted at the Doctor. 'I've seen you before.'

'About a minute ago,' the Doctor agreed.

The man shook his head. 'Short-term memory's the first to go,' he said sorrowfully.

Kari said in a low voice, 'He needs a medic.'

The man heard her, and he looked down at his scorched and damaged arm. 'I tried to pull down the control cables,' he said, 'but I picked the wrong ones. Power lines. So since I couldn't stop the buildup, I had

114

to wall it in …' he looked towards the heap of scrap. 'Only now I'm not sure I'll get it finished.'

'What buildup?' the Doctor said.

'The radiation spill. I used to monitor the levels. My name's Bor. Every time it gets worse, the forbidden zone gets bigger. But this time it's more serious.'

'In what way?'

Bor weakly indicated all around them. 'These are the engines of the old Terminus ship,' he said. 'Know what would happen if one of these exploded?'

'We'd be in big trouble,' Kari said. 'They don't just explode, they chain-react.'

Bor looked at the globe above. 'That's how this one went,' he said.

'I don't think so,' the Doctor said gently. 'The ship wouldn't still be here.'

Kari added, 'None of us would.'

'Oh,' Bor said airily, 'it was a long time ago. And the ship was protected, that's the point.'

'This is very interesting,' the Doctor said, 'but …'

Bor didn't seem to hear. He was looking at his scrapheap again. 'That one'll go next. The crack's always been there, but the leak's been getting worse. I didn't find out why until I followed the control cables.'

Valgard was thinking that he'd heard enough.

He'd been standing in the shadows at the end of the row for most of the conversation, and any doubts that he may have had were now gone. Not that it mattered; the object of the exercise was to return from the zone with evidence that he'd carried out his unwelcome job so that he could watch Eirak wriggle and squirm and try to get out of the bet that he'd made. He probably had no intention of carrying out his part of the bargain, in which case Valgard was going to see to it

115

that his authority in the Terminus would be ended forever. If you couldn't believe his promises, why believe in his threats anymore?

For now, speed was the main problem. Valgard needed to get back as quickly as possible to minimise the effects of the zone and give himself the best chance of fighting them off. He was running on the effects of a Hydromel high, brought on by the use of more than half of the drug remaining from his last issue. What remained couldn't keep him going for much longer.

He stepped out into the light. 'Tell them nothing, Bor!' he shouted. 'They're company spies!'

Bor's expression changed in an instant. 'You're from the company?' he said, horrified. 'You seemed so friendly!'

The Doctor and Kari both stood. 'They've got great respect for their employers,' the Doctor observed.

Valgard stepped out for a closer look at Bor. It was the first view he'd had of Bor's condition. 'You've been torturing him!' he accused.

'Have they?' Bor said. 'I can't remember ...'

Valgard was still advancing on them, his staff held crosswise. As they both remembered, he could use it to good effect. Kari brought her burner around, but Valgard wasn't to be fooled.

'You've no power for that,' he said. 'I was there when you found out, remember?'

Valgard kept on coming. He changed his grip on the staff, holding it out to full length and sweeping it from side to side. 'I'm taking you back for Eirak to see,' he said.

'Fine,' the Doctor said, 'Let's go. There's no need for violence.'

'That comes later. When we've finished

116

questioning you.'

'Ah. I see. In that case ...'

He seemed to be about to turn away – at least, that's how Valgard read it, which was what the Doctor had intended. On the next sweep of the staff he turned suddenly and caught the end with both hands.

For a moment, it was stalemate. With no central pivot to give the staff leverage, they were in a contest of strength, a contest that the Doctor won.

Valgard was whipped aside. The weight of his own armour kept him going, and he spun into the junk that Bor had heaped before the cracked reactor globe. With an almost deafening sound, the junk came down with Valgard sprawling in the middle of it.

'My wall!' Bor shouted in agony as he got to his feet, but he was drowned out by Valgard's screams as a beam of unchecked radiance burst from the globe. Valgard rolled aside. Bor arrived and, again using his arm to shield his face, attempted to pile some of it back.

'Well done,' Kari said approvingly, but the Doctor could get no pleasure from the victory.

'He's not as strong as he looks,' he said. 'Let's go.'

They turned to leave, but it wasn't going to be so easy. The darkness that blocked their way was huge and powerful, and its eyes glowed a dull red.

Force of habit had Kari reaching for her useless burner. 'What is it?' she said.

The massive beast was unmoving. Valgard had recovered sufficiently to prop himself up, and he said, 'You ought to know. Your people brought it here.'

'We weren't sent by the company,' the Doctor said. He was beginning to get irritated at the persistence of

Valgard's misunderstanding.

It lifted one immense paw. It took them a moment to realise that it was pointing at Bor.

'It wants something,' Kari said, although she couldn't make out what.

'It wants Bor,' Valgard said from the floor. 'It's been ordered to find him and take him back.'

'Let it pass,' the Doctor suggested to Kari. Slowly, cautiously, they moved aside. The Garm moved towards Bor. For all its size, it moved in total silence.

'Look at that skin,' the Doctor said as it passed them. 'Like natural armour.'

Kari tried to make it out. The Garm just seemed to soak up the light. 'Radiation-resistant?' she said.

'A purpose-built slave to work in the danger area.'

The Garm raised Bor from the floor as if he weighed no more than a handful of paper. Bor hung there limply, without the strength to fight or resist. But then as he was turning, the Garm stopped.

Nobody really heard it, but they all felt it: a deep stirring that was beyond sound and almost beyond sensation. 'Subsonics,' the Doctor said, adding as the Garm moved out with Bor, 'obviously some kind of signal.'

A moment later, and the beast was gone.

Kari looked at Valgard. He stared back defiantly, although he still didn't seem able to make it up from the floor. She said, 'What about him?'

'Leave him,' the Doctor said.

'I should kill him.'

'He's too weak to follow us. Come on.'

The Doctor set out with some obvious sense of purpose. He was scanning the walls and the open latticework of the ceiling above. She had to catch up

118

before she could ask, 'What are you looking for?'

'Control lines,' the Doctor explained, but when he glanced at Kari she was looking blank. 'The ones that Bor said he followed.'

Contrary to Eirak's hopes, Nyssa had been giving them a hard time.

She'd already made one attempt to run as they'd escorted her to the storeyard, and but for the fact that she turned into a blind alley between two fuel tanks, they'd have lost her. Sigurd cursed himself and kept a tight grip on her from then on. Some day soon Eirak might be selecting someone else to lose his Hydromel supply, and Sigurd didn't want to be the next in line.

They had a procedure for tethering rebellious Lazars in the storeyard, although it was more often used for those who were dazed and liable to wander if not watched. Sigurd warned his companion to hold onto Nyssa as he set off the subsonic signal and then prepared the manacle that would lock her to the supporting strut until the Garm arrived. When he turned around, his companion was on the floor and Nyssa was running again.

She wasn't at her best, but neither were they. Sickness slowed her, and heavy armour slowed them. The gap widened as she ran for the tarpaulin and ducked under. Almost immediately, Nyssa bounced back with the breath knocked out of her.

The Vanir with whom she'd collided helped them to bring her back, but for the moment she had no fight left. They lifted her and closed the self-adjusting pressure catch of the manacle around her wrist, and only then did Sigurd release his hold on her. Two bad moments like that were enough to ruin anybody's day.

He signalled his thanks to the Vanir who had helped.

'Who's team are you on,' he said, 'Gylfi's?'

The Vanir inclined his head in agreement, but further conversation was prevented as Sigurd's companion called for their attention.

'It's Bor!' he said. 'The Garm found Bor!'

The Garm came striding from the Terminus with Bor held out before. They ran to the yellow line to receive him, and when the Garm had been relieved of the body he stepped back to wait.

Bor was lowered to the floor. 'Most kind,' he was mumbling, 'most kind ...'

'The armour's ruined,' Sigurd's companion observed. The Vanir who had arrived in time to help with the capture of Nyssa stayed well back.

Sigurd said, 'We'd better get him to Eirak while he can still talk. Otherwise they'll think we stole the best parts.'

Looking at Bor now, it was difficult to see why anybody should want his armour – but Sigurd was taking no chances. He undid Bor's makeshift sling and they each got an arm around their shoulders to carry him away, feet dragging along the floor. 'Stay and watch her,' he said to the other Vanir as they passed, and a few seconds later they were gone.

The Garm was still waiting. The Vanir turned to Nyssa and said, 'Let's see that chain.'

He reached for the manacle. Nyssa tried to push him away with her free hand. It wasn't what he was expecting. He took a surprised pace back, and then he quickly removed his radiation helmet.

'It's me, Nyssa!' Olvir said.

When he'd realised what was happening he'd tried to follow and rescue her from the drone, but by that

120

time she was already being handed over to the Vanir. He'd dodged around corners twice to avoid Sigurd on his way to and from the collection of the Hydromel, and then when he'd arrived on the receiving platform it had been just in time to see the elevator dropping away. He'd followed it down by the stairs and catwalks, and stayed in the shadows as he tried to get some idea of how the Terminus was being run. His observations led him to the unattended equipment store, and there he'd been able to assemble for himself a disguise that would allow him to move around unchallenged.

The Garm was starting to move towards them. 'You'd better make this fast,' Nyssa said.

But it wasn't going to be easy. The manacle had been closed by some kind of sprung clip. It would take a lot more strength to open it than Olvir could muster.

'Don't worry,' he reassured her, 'I'll stop him.' He took a couple of steps back, reaching under his Vanir cloak as he went. He brought out his burner and levelled it at the Garm. He set it for low heat and high energy, the brick-wall effect that came out in a single concentrated zap.

It might have been a paper cup full of water. The Garm didn't even slow down. Olvir switched to a concentrated burn – humane impulses were all very well, but the situation was getting away from him – and tried again.

Nothing. He had to end the burn abruptly because the Garm was too close to Nyssa and she was at risk. The thing must have had skin like a rock. It reached out and sprang the manacle in a single easy gesture, and then swept Nyssa off the ground before she could even react.

121

He was carrying her away, into the Terminus. There was nothing that Olvir could do about it.

'I'll think of something else,' he called after her.

At least, he would try.

'Nothing,' Turlough said as he threw the last of the switches. With a few inconsequential exceptions, none of them had any effect. They could lower the control room lights or boost the air-conditioning, but they could neither get out of the ship nor let others in.

Tegan said, 'Everything's routed through the automatic pilot.'

'So we're stuck here until that box decides to let us out?'

'We don't have any choice.'

'I think we do,' Turlough said, and Tegan sensed that he was finally getting around to explain what had been bothering him for some time. 'I think there's a way we can get back to the TARDIS.'

'It would be more practical to find the Doctor.'

Turlough shook his head. 'Not at all. It would be more practical to re-create the door we came through. Wait here.'

He walked out of the control room with an obvious sense of purpose. Confused, Tegan watched him go. Whatever was going through his mind, he didn't seem ready to share it.

As soon as Turlough was certain that Tegan wasn't following, he took the communication cube from his pocket. He was fairly sure that he couldn't be overheard.

The Black Guardian came through immediately. '*You have not destroyed the Doctor,*' the cube pulsed, the ferocity of its glow an accusation.

'I haven't found him yet.'

The cube gave an intense, spasmodic surge, showing a capability Turlough hadn't been aware of. He tried to resist the wrenching pain that came with it, but he couldn't prevent himself from crying out.

'*Kill the Doctor!*' the Black Guardian urged, and the agony stayed for several seconds longer. Turlough fought not to cry out again. Tegan might hear and come to see what was happening. If she did, and if his secret was uncovered, he knew what the cube's next order would be.

'I'll do it,' he gasped as the glow died and the pain receded. 'I have a plan.'

'*You have nothing.*'

'I do. But I need to get back to the TARDIS.'

'*Why?*'

'Trust me,' he pleaded, knowing that he had little chance, and it was then that he heard Tegan calling. She must have heard something. Quickly, he went on, 'How do I recreate the door?'

'*Fail me again...* the Black Guardian said ominously, but Turlough did his best to put a confidence into his voice that he didn't feel.

'I won't, I promise. But how do I get back?'

'*You have skills, use them. Look beneath your feet.*'

Underfoot? What could he have seen under the floor that would give him a clue to the way back to the TARDIS? He tried to think through the stages which had led to the creation of the door: the breakup, the emergency programme set to home in on the distinctive radiation waveform of a passing ship...

Tegan was coming around the corner. He realised that he still had the communication cube in his hand, and he quickly pocketed it.

He thought he had an answer.

Tegan was looking puzzled. She'd been expecting to find him in some kind of trouble. 'What are you doing?' she said.

'I need you to help me. We've got to find the place where the door to the TARDIS appeared, and then we've got to find a way of lifting one of the floor panels.'

'But why?'

'I'll explain when we get there.'

The catwalks deep inside the Terminus were considerably different to those that had been added by the Vanir and by their immediate predecessors; these had been built for bodies with dimensions that were decidedly non-human. It wasn't as difficult as the Doctor expected to find the lines that Bor had identified as power and control cables, because his tracks were fresh in the dust. It seemed that the Garm kept to his own areas, and they didn't include anywhere above floor-level.

The lines and cables were colour-coded, and they ran parallel to the walk. Kari couldn't understand why they were following – literally – in Bor's footsteps at all. 'But what's the point?' she said. 'He's crazy.'

'Crazy to think he could make an effective radiation shield out of junk, yes,' the Doctor conceded. 'But he knew what he was talking about.'

'I wish I did.'

'They're using a leaky containment drive as a kill-or-cure, that's risky enough. If we don't get out of here soon, we'll glow in the dark for the rest of our lives.' The Doctor was hardly exaggerating. With access to the facilities in the TARDIS, he was confident that he could reverse the effects of mild radiation contamination. It was a fairly simple case of rigging a low-power matter transmitter with a discriminating filter between the two ends. But when the contamination had been around for long enough to cause actual cell damage on a detectable scale, there was no way of reversing the process.

'But you think there's an even bigger danger than that?' Kari said.

'Bor seemed to think so. Follow these lines, and we'll find out why.'

They carried Bor into the Vanir's converted storage tank and laid him on one of the bunks. He was weak, and he was starting to become delirious again after a brief period of lucidity. Someone was sent to get Eirak, and Sigurd crouched by the bunk.

'You hear me, old man?' he said.

Bor stared at the ceiling. 'Sigurd?'

'Why did you do it? You knew you wouldn't last.'

'Worth a try ... the pilot's dead, you know.'

'Which pilot?'

'Pilot of the Terminus.'

Now he was definitely rambling. The Terminus hadn't moved under its own power or anything else's for generations. Sigurd said, 'The pilot's dead and long gone.'

'Oh, no,' Bor insisted, 'he's still there. But he's going to fire up the engines, and they won't take it.'

There was a noise from behind. Sigurd looked up to see Eirak on his way over from the door. He came and stood by the bunk, and glanced from one end to the other. 'Where's his helmet?' he said making no attempt to lower his voice.

'He didn't have it.'

Eirak inspected Bor's ruined armour critically. 'Did he say why he went into the zone?'

Sigurd shook his head. 'I can't make sense of it.'

'Well …' Eirak straightened. 'One less on the rosters.'

Seeing that the watch-commander was about to leave without further comment, Sigurd said, 'But he needs Hydromel!'

The answer was harsh and direct. 'There isn't any to spare.'

'But he's dying!'

'So why detain him?' Eirak said curtly, and he walked away.

The Doctor and Kari had followed the control cables to their end; they led to the control chamber of the Terminus ship.

It wasn't easy to get in. The floor and the ceiling had been built on a slope, so there was hardly enough headroom. A recess had been cut into the slope for the central control couch, and all of the controls and displays had been packed into the available space around this. It didn't leave much space to move around.

Not that the pilot needed any. He was most definitely dead.

The suited body in the couch was half as big again as a man, its contorted alien face half-hidden by the tinted bubble of a pressure helmet. As the Doctor crouched and moved across for a closer look, he could make out only a few details by the lights of the live instrumentation. They gave the alien the look of the screaming skull design that had been painted on the

126

outside of the Terminus ship's hull.

It seemed all wrong. The place didn't have the feeling of long-ago disaster that he'd been expecting. Something had gone wrong – the dead pilot and the damaged reactor globe down in the engine section were evidence of that – but from what he could see around him, the Doctor would have guessed that all of this had happened only hours before. And that, of course, was impossible.

Kari seemed fascinated by the dim vision of horror that could be made out through the alien's visor glass. Squeezing himself between units for a closer look at a part of the console, the Doctor said, 'Do you remember Bor telling us that one of the Terminus engines had exploded?'

'Did he?' Kari said, only half-aware.

'Look at this panel.' he pointed, and Kari had to shake herself to concentrate. The Doctor went on, 'The Terminus was once capable of time travel.'

She stared. The layout meant nothing to her. She was combat section. She said, 'So?'

'To push a ship of this size through time would take an enormous amount of energy.'

'What are you getting at?'

'Think about what we've learned. The Terminus seems to be at the centre of the known universe. Imagine the ship in flight. Suddenly the pilot finds that he has a vast amount of unstable reaction mass on board. What would you do?'

Kari didn't have to think it over. 'I'd jettison. It's the only answer.'

'And a perfectly normal procedure, under more conventional circumstances. Unfortunately, this pilot ejected his fuel into a void.'

127

'And it exploded.'

'Starting a chain reaction which led to Event One.'

It took a moment for Kari to grasp what was being said, but then her eyes widened in amazement. 'The Big Bang?' she said. 'But why wasn't the Terminus destroyed?'

'As Bor said, it was protected. The pilot used a low-power time-hopper to jump the ship forward a few hours, leaving the unstable fuel behind to burn itself out. He obviously thought it would be a localised reaction and no danger to anybody. Unfortunately, the chain reaction just got bigger and bigger ... the shockwave must have caught up with him and boosted the ship billions of years into the future.'

'And killed the pilot.'

'As well as damaging a second engine. Which is still active.'

Kari looked again at the pilot, this time with even greater awe. He was more than an alien; he was the last survivor of a universe which he'd destroyed with his error, and his dying moments had been spent looking on the new universe that he'd inadvertently brought into being in its place.

But if the second engine was still active ... didn't that mean that the whole process could take place again?

The Doctor was staring at one of the console controls. 'Did you see anything move?' he said.

'I haven't been looking. why?'

'Something's changed, and I'm not sure what.' He seemed to be looking most intently at a T-shaped control handle that was almost within the reach of the pilot's gloved hand. The three-fingered claw lay on the panel, actually touching nothing.

But as they watched, the handle moved a fraction.

'A pre-ignition sequence!' the Doctor said. 'It's already been programmed in!'

'But he couldn't. He's dead!'

'The ship doesn't know that. It'll go ahead anyway. We've got to try to shut the damaged engine down.'

'But how?'

'Well,' the Doctor said, shifting himself around to reach across the control panel, 'we can start by seeing if we can reset that handle.'

Olvir tried to get ahead of the Garm, but he hadn't counted on the labyrinthine complexity of the Terminus interior. He couldn't effectively make his way alone, and when he tried to retrace his steps the Garm had, of course, moved on. He listened, but the beast made no sound. It was only Nyssa's weak calling of his name that gave him something to follow. He caught up just as Nyssa was being strapped to an upright before the damaged reactor globe of the ship's engines.

He saw Bor's junkheap. More important, he saw the deadly crack that was only partly covered, light streaming through like the gaze of Satan. Nyssa called his name again, and Olvir started forward.

If he hadn't still been wearing Vanir armour, walking into Valgard's staff might have killed him.

Olvir folded, all the breath smacked out of him. He felt as if he'd been rammed in the midsection by a truck. He hit the floor, sack-like and out of control, as the Garm ambled across his lurching field of vision towards the stacked machine parts. Olvir wondered with a detached kind of curiosity what might be coming next. For the moment, he had only the most tenuous contact with his body and his surroundings. He tried to focus on the Garm, but Valgard got in the way.

'Where are the others?' he demanded, hefting his staff ready for another blow.

'What?' Sensation was returning to Olvir now, and its return was bad news.

'The other spies!' Cheated of prey once, Valgard wasn't going to allow Olvir any advantages. The staff came down towards Olvir's head in a bone-splitting hammer-blow. Olvir ducked, took some of the force on his protected shoulder, and slid up under the rod to grab hold of Valgard. The staff was useless for close-up fighting, and it was here that Olvir would have the edge of youth and strength.

It wasn't the bonus that he'd hoped. Valgard had over-ridden the metering mechanism on the intra-venous Hydromel dispenser that was fixed to the chestplate of his armour, and he'd used up all of his reserves in a single shot. For a while, at least, he would feel immortal. Olvir tried some of his best moves, the ones that had won him points in combat training, but Valgard blocked them all. They spun and they circled, and Olvir had little chance to register what the Garm might be doing.

Valgard tried to break free to make a useful distance for his staff, but Olvir wouldn't let him. Olvir tried to bring his burner around for a close shot, but Valgard knocked it to the floor and kicked it away. They swung around again. Olvir could see that the Garm was leaning hard against the side of the junkheap.

The animal bulldozed the scrap aside. Radiant light burst through, and Nyssa was directly in its path. She

130

screamed.

Olvir suddenly switched tactics. Instead of pulling away, he launched himself onto Valgard. The Vanir suddenly found that he was trying to hold the combined weight of Olvir and two sets of armour.

Given warning, he might just have managed it. He swayed for several seconds, but he was already beaten. He crashed to the ground with Olvir on top of him.

They rolled apart, winded. Olvir was feeling sick and dizzy at this, his second hand-out of abuse, but he struggled to his knees. If only he wasn't too late. He had to get Nyssa away from the danger of the radiation field.

But Nyssa was no longer there.

Olvir stared mutely at the chain and the straps that had secured her. They swung gently in the deadly light. He made it onto his feet. There was no sign of the Garm, either, and no clue as to where they might have gone. His burner had come to rest close to the reactor globe – too close for safety. He'd have to reach into the hottest part of the danger area in order to reach it.

'I wouldn't,' Valgard said from behind him. 'The radiation would kill you.'

Olvir turned. Valgard was still on the floor where he'd fallen, but he'd managed to prop himself up. He said, 'Get much closer and you're dead, unless you can get to a decontamination unit.'

'You're lying.'

Valgard shrugged. 'Go ahead, then. In my day we had better training.'

'What are you talking about?'

'You're a raider, aren't you? Combat trained.

131

Colonel Periera, was it? The one they call the Chief?'

Olvir tried not to let his surprise show, but it was unavoidable. He said, 'How do you know?'

Valgard shifted a little in an attempt to make the most of the strength that he had left. 'I recognise the moves,' he said. 'He taught the same ones to me. I was with him for five tours until he turned me in for the reward.' He shook his head, and smiled at the memory. 'I was lining up to do the same to him, but he beat me to it. Good times.'

'How did you get here?'

'We're slave labour, all of us. That's how the Terminus works.'

'Where are the guards?'

Valgard almost laughed. 'Don't need them. If we don't work, there's no Hydromel for us.' He put out a hand. 'Help me up,' he said, but there was a whining note in his voice that caused Olvir to step back a little further.

'Come on,' Valgard said, 'Look at me. I'm a danger to nobody. I'm finished and I'm dying.'

But Olvir wasn't to be won around. He said, 'Where did that thing take Nyssa?'

'Who?'

'The girl. Where did it take her?'

'I don't know. This is the first time I've ever been into the zone.'

'Will he harm her?'

'He's supposed to be helping her to get cured. That's what he's here for.'

Olvir glanced across at the straps and chains. They'd stopped swinging. If this was Valgard's idea of a healing process, he'd got it badly wrong. Was it worth even attempting to find Nyssa if she was

132

doomed anyway?

He said, 'How can this be expected to cure anybody?'

'Help me, and I'll show you.' Valgard was just a little too eager in his offer. Olvir didn't believe that the Vanir knew any more about the inner workings of the Terminus than he did.

Olvir said, 'I'll find her myself.' The Garm hadn't passed them as they'd fought, so that limited the choice of directions. Olvir took a guess and moved off.

'Don't leave me,' Valgard called after him.

One of the tactical principles of the Chief's combat training programme was that no enemy should be left alive if there was a possibility that he could pose a future threat. Olvir obviously thought that Valgard was finished and not worth the attention... which was what Valgard had wanted him to think.

As soon as he was sure that Olvir had gone, the Vanir scrambled to his feet. He wasn't fast, but he was a long way from being the helpless invalid that he'd pretended to be as long as the young raider was around. He got his staff and went over to the reactor globe, approaching in such a way that he was out of the direct line of the radiation. The staff was his protection as he used it to draw Olvir's burner out of the danger area.

His time in the zone might be getting short, but he had a weapon. Let them try to stop him now!

'Are you all right?' Tegan said anxiously, and Turlough fanned some of the acrid smoke away. His attempts to pull down some of the shielding in the newly uncovered section of the underfloor area had started a small electrical fire, but it had quickly burned itself out.

'I'm all right,' Turlough assured her.

'I might be able to help you if you'd tell me what you're trying to do.'

'There was some kind of radiation leak around here, remember? It gets worse when the motors are running. That's when the door to the TARDIS is fully materialised... that leak must be the engine signature that the emergency programme attached itself to.' And as if to prove a point, Turlough leaned back and started to kick at the cladding which lined the underfloor tunnel. There were sparks and more smoke, but pieces of the cladding came away.

Tegan looked up. On the wall behind her, a faint ghost-image of the door to the TARDIS was starting to appear. She was about to tell Turlough, but the liner's automated warning voice beat her to it.

'*Primary ignition is now beginning,*' it boomed down the corridors. '*All systems running on test. Departure sequence is beginning now.*'

'What's happening?' Tegan said.

'I should think that's obvious. The liner's getting ready to leave.'

'But we can't leave yet!'

The liner was deaf to any argument that Tegan might offer it. '*All drones to designated assembly points,*' it went on, '*Countdown to secondary ignition follows.*'

Turlough heaved himself half-way back to corridor level, and he looked at the results of his work with some satisfaction. He estimated that the door was about one-third materialised. Tegan was no longer looking; she was more concerned about their imminent departure. They were already separated from the Doctor and Nyssa, and it was a situation that threatened to become permanent.

'The ship's on automatic,' Turlough told her. 'There's nothing you can do.'

'But I've got to try,' she said, and before he could argue any further she'd set off towards the control room.

She covered the distance in record time. As she ran, the decks beneath her feet began to rumble with the buildup of launch power. Coming into the command area stopped her short for a moment. It was a room peopled by busy ghosts, ranks of empty seats before which controls were setting themselves and read-outs were displaying to no purpose. But Tegan knew that all of this activity was only secondary, a reflection of the orders that were being issued by the automatic command centre at the forward end of the room.

'*Departure sequence is now under way*,' the box announced calmly. '*Countdown to docking disengagement is now beginning. Preparing to blow clamps and withdraw all lines.*'

She began to look for some main control or master switch, but there was nothing. 'Can anyone hear me?' she said, knowing that she was wasting her time. 'You must stop.'

'*Countdown to primary burn is now under way.*'

The deck was almost shaking.

'*Test mode on all systems is disengaged, all systems operating within permitted tolerances.*'

'Can't you shut up!' Tegan yelled in frustration, and she slammed her fist down on top of the automatics.

The control box shut up.

Tegan couldn't believe it. An alarm started ringing

somewhere, and a call of *Emergency! Launch abort* was echoing around the rest of the liner, and several lights on the control console had died whilst others were blinking furiously.

She ran back to tell Turlough. For the first time since they'd arrived, it was starting to look as if the whole messy adventure might be brought to a safe conclusion.

The floor panel was still open, but the door to the TARDIS had faded again. And it seemed that Turlough had gone with it.

The rise in engine power prior to the aborted launch had given Turlough the opportunity he needed. The underfloor leak had intensified, the door had become solid, and Turlough had wasted no time in going through. He made straight for the console room, and he set his communication cube down by the master control.

'*The Doctor still lives.*' There was no expression in the voice.

'He's powerless,' Turlough said, 'He's trapped, he's probably dead already.' He did his best to sound confident, but he could see too late that it wasn't coming through.

It would have made no difference, anyway. The Black Guardian's voice was dark with anger. '*You represent a poor investment of my time and energy,*' it said, and the brightness of the cube began to increase. '*There is only one course to follow with such an investment.*'

Without warning, the cube escalated to peak brightness. The energy explosion that followed was like that of a bottled sun breaking free.

The Doctor hadn't been having much success with the main control handle of the Terminus. He took off his jacket and tried to force it from every angle, but there seemed to be no way of moving it. Kari tried when he became exhausted, and then they combined their strength and pushed together. The only movement that the handle made was in the direction that had already been programmed in.

'Why won't it move?' Kari demanded, exasperated, as they took a couple of minutes to get their breath back.

'It's computer-controlled,' the Doctor said. He was about to add something else, but he didn't; instead, he looked over the console as if he was seeing it in the light of a new idea.

Kari knew better than to interrupt. After a few moments, the Doctor said, 'The technology here is phenomenal.'

'I don't understand why it's still functional after all this time.'

The Doctor tapped the console, thoughtfully. 'Have you heard of a timeslip?'

'No. What is it?'

'Something that can happen if you try to make a jump through time without any adequate form of control. At least, that's the theory. You arrive with your timescale way out of alignment with your surroundings; subjective time seems normal, but it's passing much more slowly in relation to everything else.'

'You mean ... the whole Terminus is on slow time?'

'A neat way of putting it. Yes, that's more or less what I mean. What we're witnessing is probably a high-speed emergency programme to deal with an unstable engine – except that it's taken several hundred years to get this far.

Kari shook her head. 'This is madness.'

'If I'm right, the time differential will make it impossible to move that lever. It would take the strength of a giant.'

'A giant?' Kari said, and their eyes met as they both had the same realisation. There was a giant already around. He took the Lazars off into the forbidden zone.

Olvir, meanwhile, had found the Garm.

Unfortunately, he seemed to have found it too late. The beast was empty-handed, and there was no sign of Nyssa anywhere. Olvir wasn't sure how best to deal with it. Intimidation was probably a waste of time, as he'd found when he failed even to sting it with his burner – and he didn't have the weapon anyway, so it was all rather academic.

He knew that it could understand at least a few rudimentary commands. Furthermore, he was wearing enough of his Vanir armour to look as if he was entitled to exercise authority. He decided to give it a try.

He stepped from the shadows before the Garm, and his nerve almost failed him. The dark beast seemed to fill the passageway, and the glowing coals that were its eyes gazed down on him and their message seemed to be, *I see through you, little man*.

'I'm unarmed,' Olvir said quickly, showing his hands. The Garm stopped. Olvir added, uncertainly, 'Can you understand me?'

'Perfectly,' the Garm said.

The voice was a shock. An inhuman, bass-magnified whisper, it seemed to come, not from the Garm, but from all around the Terminus itself. In spite of the strangeness, there was an unexpectedly gentle quality.

'Why are you doing this?' Olvir said. 'Why are you torturing people?'

'I drive the disease from them. All would die, but many survive.'

'And the last one you treated? Nyssa? Did she survive?'

'She is recovering.'

'Where?'

There was an awkward pause. Then: 'Follow me.' The Garm turned to go. Olvir, having no better ideas, did as he was told.

Bor hadn't moved from the bunk where they'd laid him. Even if he'd wanted to, he probably couldn't have managed it. Sigurd was the only one who stayed around after trading his rostered duties against a promise of extra work in the future. He'd had some absurd idea that he might be able to help. Instead, he could only witness Bor's slow defeat by the effects of an overlong stay in the zone.

'Try to relax,' he urged, as Bor stiffened with a particularly bad spasm of pain.

'It doesn't matter,' Bor gasped after a while, as the spasm ended and left him with a few moments of relief. He'd already had all of Sigurd's Hydromel, protesting at the sacrifice. 'In a couple of hours there won't even be a Terminus. Or a company. Or anything ... I found out all about it in the zone.'

'What's going to happen?'

139

'That's the trouble. I can't remember.' Bor managed a weak, wry smile. 'Short-term memory's always the first to go.'

Another spasm threatened. Bor waited it out, but for once it didn't last. Perhaps even that was a bad sign. Sigurd said, 'Look, I'll get more Hydromel.'

'Eirak won't release any.'

'Who said I was going to ask him?'

Sigurd went across to the thin curtain that divided the sleeping quarters from the larger space of the headquarters section. For all of the great size of the Terminus, the amount of usable space that was available to the Vanir had always been small. But even the best-shielded sections gave only temporary protection, and without any means of controlling the circulation of contaminated air their effect was limited.

The Hydromel container was on open view. The two chains that held it down were thin, but the real problem lay with the trembler alarms to which they were connected. Any attempt to cut them or to smash the lock would bring Eirak running. And if that happened Sigurd knew that, within a few days, there would be another Vanir lying sick and delirious on the other side of the curtain, and it would be him. Eirak could cancel his supply and make it stick. If he could order Valgard into the zone and get away with it, he could get away with anything.

'It really isn't worth the trouble, you know,' Bor called feebly from the sleeping area. And the pity of it was, Sigurd had to agree.

The Garm said nothing more, gliding along ahead of Olvir. The young raider kept his distance. Silence

140

only added to the aura of power around the beast, and Olvir could still remember how ineffectual his burner had been against its armoured skin. They'd already come down through open deck areas with strange markings drawn out on the floor, and passed through a long corridor that seemed to be lined entirely with black glass. Now they emerged about half-way down a metal gantry onto a spiralling access ramp.

The Garm led him upward. They were back in the open, and the ramp led them between vertical cooling fins several storeys high. Olvir took one look at the drop from the unguarded edge of the ramp, and wished he hadn't – the air turbulence between the fins tugged at him and tried to pull him over. The wind was nowhere near strong enough, but it was an uncomfortable feeling.

They climbed into the support structure at the top of the fins, and Olvir could see the metal-honeycomb skin of the Terminus only a few metres overhead. The ramp ended in a grillework deck that groaned slightly as the Garm's weight came onto it, seeming hardly enough to protect them from the long fall into darkness below. It began to occur to Olvir that he'd trusted the Garm too readily, but he was already so apprehensive that he didn't think it could get any worse. Besides, if the animal meant him harm, none of this would have been necessary.

In the far corner of the deck was a square tank about the size of a double cabin. It had probably been some kind of monitoring or flow-control room for the cooling fins, but now the window overlooking the drop had been covered with metal sheets spot-welded at their edges. The only other access was by a door with some kind of wheel-operated lock. The Garm raised a massive paw to indicate this. Olvir was, it seemed, where he wanted to be. Wherever it was.

He looked at the Garm and said, 'Well?' But the Garm didn't move. This was as far as it felt able to go without running against some earlier instruction. Olvir went across to the door and took a closer look. There was no provision for a key or anything like a key, so it was possible that the mechanism was just a simple catch.

This could be a problem. The simple things always were. Races sharing some part of their culture and history could take for granted such things as catches and switches and dials, whilst to outsiders they became complex puzzles. Olvir turned again to the Garm. At least he could try asking for some guidance.

But the Garm's head was turned slightly to one side as if to listen to something that no one else could hear. Olvir realised that the Vanir must be sounding the signal to bring the Garm back to the storeyard for another Lazar. As if in confirmation, the Garm turned and began to descend the ramp.

Olvir felt strangely alone. The Garm had hardly been good company, but at least it had been alive and, in spite of the surgical alterations that had been carried out to ensure its obedience, it had seemed intelligent. Doing the best that he could to fight the solitary feeling, Olvir set to work on the catch.

It didn't take as long as he'd feared. It was simply a case of performing two operations at the same time, and the door swung open. As Olvir stepped forward, hands grabbed him and jerked him roughly inside.

Taken off-balance, the weight of his armour brought him crashing to the floor. He had an impression of dazzling whiteness and a dark shape poised over him and ready to strike. *I'm glad Kari didn't see this*, he was thinking, *what an embarrassing way to go*.

But then vision started to clear, and the dark shape filled out with detail as its small fist was slowly lowered.

'Olvir!' Nyssa said. 'What are you doing here?'

She climbed off his chest and let him sit up, blinking at the brightness of the room. It had been tiled in white throughout, and there was some kind of pulsing illumination from above that gave off a faint ozone smell.

There was also something else; Nyssa was showing none of the signs of the Lazar disease.

Olvir said, 'You came through the cure?'

'Just about,' Nyssa said, and from her expression it had been a pretty grim process.

'What happened?'

'Just a massive dose of radiation and nothing else. There's no proper diagnosis, no control.' She gestured around. 'And this is supposed to be someone's idea of decontamination.'

Olvir got to his feet. 'Let's go,' he said. 'The sooner we can put the Terminus behind us ...'

'You don't understand! There must be thousands of people who've passed through here and think they're cured. It's all just hit and miss. Nobody cares.'

Olvir tried to get her towards the door, but she wouldn't be distracted. 'Listen to me,' she went on urgently. 'The cure works, but it has to be controlled. Otherwise you just trade one killer for another! Radiation-induced diseases that may take years to show!'

'All right!' Olvir said firmly. This was a rescue, and

143

the rights and wrongs could be argued out later. 'Let's concentrate on getting away.'

Nyssa allowed herself to be ushered towards the outside. 'It could all be changed,' she said as they stepped out onto the decking.

'I don't doubt it,' Olvir assured her. 'But for now, we've got a lot of ground to cover.'

The Vanir hadn't given the signal for the Garm. The Doctor had.

The small box housing the subsonic generator had been fixed to its upright by a couple of bolts, and removing it hadn't been a problem. The Vanir might have a back-up, but after seeing the rest of their shoestring operation, he doubted it. Without the box the Vanir couldn't recall the Garm; with it, the Doctor and Kari had the exclusive use of the animal's strength.

The Doctor's main fear at the moment was that Eirak and the others might arrive before the Garm did. It was unlikely that they'd hear the signal at any distance – the Garm probably had an implanted receptor somewhere at the base of its brain for that – but it would soon be time for the next Lazar transfer.

Kari stood at the pick-up point. She'd found some white dust and used it to give herself something of the pale complexion of a Lazar, but under the make-up she was drained and nervous anyway. At least she wouldn't have to worry about the disease itself, if the Doctor's theory about a narrow-range virus was right; although radioactively foul, the Terminus would be clean as far as the disease-causing organism was concerned. The evidence was there in the Vanir. For all of their close contact with the sick, none of them showed any signs of joining them. They had other problems.

Kari glanced at the Doctor. 'You're sure this will work?' she said.

The Doctor gave her a confident smile. 'Trust me,' he said. And he thought to himself, *I hope I don't regret this ...*

The Garm was with them before they knew it. He emerged from the shadows as smoothly as a dark sunrise and then he hesitated, looking from one to the other as if he was unsure of what to do next.

'Go!' the Doctor urged. The plan was that Kari should retreat before the Garm, leading him back towards the Terminus control room. The Doctor would follow with the subsonic generator, ready to use it as a crude training-aid if it should be necessary.

But Kari said, stiff and panicky, 'I can't remember the way.'

'Deception is unnecessary,' the Garm told them, and the Doctor and Kari exchanged a look of astonishment. 'You've given the signal. I have no choice but to obey.'

It was a relief to put the storeyard behind them. An appearance by Eirak and the others at this late stage would at best delay them, and time was already impossibly short. The line which marked the edge of the forbidden zone was a paradoxical indicator of their safety.

The Doctor led the way, following the control cables again to the bridge of the Terminus. The Garm hesitated a little when faced with an ascent into areas that it had never seen before, but the persuasion of the subsonics over-rode everything else.

145

Just as they were coming level with the point where Bor had attempted to damage the lines and had instead succeeded in damaging himself, the whole of the Terminus seemed to give a distinct tremble. It happened again as they reached the control room, as if the whole massive structure of the ship was beginning to absorb the strain of the forces that were to come. The Doctor wondered for how long the Terminus might hold out. Would it be destroyed in the blast along with everything else, or would it make another one-way leap into nowhere on the crest of the shockwave? Either way, they'd never know.

The Garm had trouble fitting into the narrow space of the control room. The Doctor saw with alarm that the handle had almost completed its closure. They had minutes, at the most. He hurriedly explained what he wanted the Garm to do, feeling precious time slip by as he talked.

The Garm looked at the handle. It jerked down another fraction.

'I'd appreciate it if you'd hurry,' the Doctor said.

The Garm turned the glow of its eyes onto him. 'This is necessary?'

'If you can return the handle, I can disconnect the circuitry controlling it.'

'And if I fail?'

'Don't fail.'

The Garm positioned itself with a hand clamped over the handle and its back against the rear wall of the control room. It overshadowed the dead pilot, making him seem like some grotesque doll. First it tested the resistance of the control. Unsatisfied, it shifted position slightly. Then it threw all of its strength into a single, powered effort. There was a

146

sound like old leather creaking, like bundles of cane being twisted together, and the Doctor quickly slid around in order to get to the contacts that were under the console surface.

There wouldn't be any time for elaborate work, and even if there had been the Doctor lacked the necessary familiarity with the design. What he intended was a more precise version of what Bor had tried to do. Bor's mistake had been in trying to disconnect the controls when the process was already too far along to be reversed. First the main handle had to be returned – which was why they needed the Garm – and then the contacts could be broken so that the engines could never again be returned to their dangerous state.

But the handle wasn't moving.

The Garm seemed to have stopped its descent, but that was all. The Terminus was vibrating again, an earthquake that rippled through the floors and walls and echoed in all the open spaces. Stopping the handle just wasn't enough.

'You have to push harder,' the Doctor said.

Without wavering, the Garm raised its head. Its bright eyes fixed on the Doctor. 'It's the only way,' he said quietly, knowing that he was asking the Garm to go to the limits of its strength and beyond. He also knew of the savagely unfair advantage that possession of the subsonic control had given him.

'Please,' Kari said.

The Garm bent its head, and made another and greater effort.

The handle started to move.

It was slow at first, but then the Garm started to pour on the power and make the most of its success.

The Doctor waited as long as he dared and then started to pull out handfuls of wiring; he'd already chosen the areas that he wanted to disconnect, and he hoped that the flashing and the smoke from under the console wouldn't make him miss anything.

'That's it!' he said at last. The Garm had been holding the handle hard against its backstop. For a moment, it seemed unable to release itself from the strain. Then, with the suddenness of a collapsing fire, it fell back.

The handle didn't move. They listened. The Terminus was still.

'Have I served you well?' The Garm was exhausted.

'You certainly have,' the Doctor told it.

'Then do something for me.'

'Name it.'

'Destroy the box. Set me free.'

The Doctor didn't even need to weigh the arguments for and against. He dropped the signal box onto the floor and stepped on it, hard. It made a satisfying crunching noise under his heel.

'Rest,' he told the Garm. 'You've earned it.' And then he glanced at a relieved-looking Kari and indicated that they should leave the control room.

'Now what?' she said on the approach walk outside.

'We finish what Bor started. If we break the control lines, we'll be making double-sure that this can't happen again.'

But it wasn't going to be so easy. They knew as much when they saw Valgard at the far end of the catwalk, grinning like a madman. Olvir's burner was in his hands, and it was covering them.

'Look,' the Doctor said, 'whoever you are, we haven't got time for this.' Kari said nothing; she was

148

staring at the burner, wondering what its loss might imply for Olvir.

'Just carry on down,' Valgard said, and he used the muzzle of the burner to usher them towards the descent.

'You're taking a very narrow view of this,' the Doctor told him as they reached the base level and moved over towards the main tunnel, but Valgard wasn't impressed.

'I want to stay alive,' he said. 'If that's a narrow view, then you're right.'

They moved down the broad walk with shadows all around. The overhead lights mapped out the way ahead, a series of isolated pools. The Doctor said, 'And you're happy to see things go on as they are?'

'Happy?' Valgard echoed bitterly. 'This is the Terminus. Nobody's happy here. Staying alive is all that counts.'

'Things could change,' the Doctor suggested, but he wasn't too hopeful. All of Valgard's mind was concentrated on his own survival, and he wasn't open to any new ideas that didn't appear to fit in.

It was over in seconds. There was a shout from somewhere in the darkness, Valgard spun around to cover himself against a possible attack, and Olvir rammed him squarely between the shoulders from behind. Valgard toppled like a broken statue, and the burner skidded out of his hands to land almost at Kari's feet. She had it levelled in less than a second.

'Just freeze,' she told Valgard, and he abandoned any idea of resistance.

Olvir picked himself up, and Nyssa came forward out of the shadows. The Doctor's relief and delight at seeing her safe was evident.

'I'm fine,' she assured him, 'but listen. I've discovered something. They're using crude radiation to cure the Lazar disease.'

'I suspected something like it.'

'But the system they use is nearly as dangerous. There's got to be some way of making the Terminus company understand.'

'You've thought of a better way?'

'Ask the Garm. He's used to handling radiation, but they just treat him like a slave. You know he can't do anything of his own free will?'

The Doctor was about to tell her that the Garm had been released from the influence of the subsonic generator, but Valgard beat him to it.

'She's sick,' he said. 'She doesn't know what she's talking about.'

Nyssa turned to him, making her point with such force that he flinched. 'With changes the Terminus could work,' she insisted. 'It could be a decent hospital.'

Valgard shook his head, wearied by what he considered to be her excessive optimism. 'The company isn't interested.'

'No? And what about you? What about the other Vanir?'

'That doesn't make any difference. We can't do anything without Hydromel, and the company controls the supply.'

'But if you could get it from somewhere else, you'd be free of their control, wouldn't you?'

Valgard stared, awe mixing with a tiny dash of hope. She *means* it! he thought.

Bor would swing from one extreme to the other. A

moment ago he had been incoherent, but now he was lucid.

'Am I dead yet?' he said. He sounded puzzled.

Sigurd returned to his side, a half-filled cup of water in his hand in case Bor should need it. 'No,' he said.

'Funny. I could have sworn ...' Whatever he was going to say, Bor put it from his mind and brightened up a little. 'Still, it's a relief. I'm hoping for something rather better on the other side.' He frowned. 'Sigurd?'

'Try to sleep.'

'Sleep! It's all I can do to ... stay awake for more than a minute ...'

Sigurd stood, and looked down at Bor with sad compassion. This will be the end of us all, he was thinking. Thank you, Terminus Incorporated. Thanks for nothing.

There was movement on the other side of the curtain, people entering the tank. Probably Eirak and the others taking a shift break. Sigurd went through, and came face to face with Valgard.

He motioned to Sigurd to be quiet. He was slightly flushed and his eyes were like flinty points, certain signs of a Hydromel high. He said, 'I've got some people with me.'

Sigurd watched, bewildered, as a line of strangers came trooping into the converted tank. The Doctor was first in line, and he went straight to the Hydromel case. Nyssa, Kari and Olvir gathered around him. 'I assume this is it,' he said.

'Now, wait a minute,' Sigurd said, pushing his way through the group, but Valgard's hand landed on his shoulder and held him back. The Doctor was already crouching for a closer look at the trembler alarms.

'They say they can free us from the company,'

Valgard told him.

'You believe that?'

'You know anybody harder to convince?'

The chains were already off, the alarms disabled. 'Burner, please,' the Doctor said, and Olvir handed the weapon over.

Sigurd said. 'If this is just some madcap scheme for getting back at Eirak ...'

The lock of the Hydromel case was vaporised in a moment, and the Doctor lifted the lid. He removed a phial and handed it to Nyssa.

'You're the expert,' he said. 'What do you think?'

She inspected it against the light, and then twisted off the glass seal and gave a cautious sniff. As she was doing this, the Doctor turned to Kari and said in a low voice, 'While we're sorting things out here, perhaps the two of you would like to go back and finish Bor's work on the control lines.'

Kari nodded, Olvir retrieved his burner, and the two of them left in silence. Nyssa, meanwhile, had completed her brief inspection of the Hydromel.

'It's crude stuff,' she said. 'Probably organic.'

'Can you synthesise it?' the Doctor asked.

'I can probably improve on it.'

Sigurd still wasn't convinced, and he was determined not to be ignored. He said, 'How's this supposed to free us from the company?'

Nyssa explained it patiently, as if to a child. 'Terminus Incorporated only control you because they supply you with Hydromel. But if you produced your own ...'

'Here on the Terminus,' Valgard added, and Sigurd suddenly grasped the idea.

'Is it possible?' he said.

Nyssa gave him a pained look, as if he was doubting her abilities. 'Of course. The company won't be able to do a thing about it. Who's going to risk coming here to argue?'

There was a groan from Bor, over on the other side of the tank. Sigurd glanced over, and then he grabbed one of the Hydromel phials from the case. 'I'm with you,' he said, and then he hurried over to attend to Bor.

Eirak had been a little perturbed by the shudders that had gone through the frame of the Terminus ship, but he'd thought them nothing new. Some of the liner dockings could be clumsy and rough, and would produce the same effect, and the same must be true of some of the so-called 'clean boats'. Nobody amongst the Vanir knew what happened to the Lazars once the Garm had taken them away, but it seemed a safe assumption that an infection-free shuttle must dock at some other point to take away the cured ... or the dead.

No, Terminus-quakes were nothing new. These were bigger than most, but Eirak was distracted by another preoccupation – the disappearance of the subsonic generator.

'I want it found,' he was saying yet again as he entered the headquarters tank, and a couple of the Vanir trailed along behind in the hope that he might be able to give them some practical suggestion on how to go about this. 'Without it, there's not a thing we can ...' He tailed off as he saw Valgard.

'Pleased to see me?' Valgard said. 'I want you to meet some people.'

The Doctor and Nyssa nodded amiably. They stood

153

one to each side of the Hydromel container. Eirak could see that it was open.

'All right, Valgard,' he said. 'What do you think you're doing?'

'I think you owe me something,' Valgard said, and as he spoke Sigurd and Bor emerged from the bunkhouse section of the tank. Bor was sick-looking, but with the Hydromel's help he could stand. He had a blanket wrapped around his shoulders.

Sigurd said, 'We'd like to talk about the small matter of your position here.'

'"Bring back the intruders"', Valgard quoted, '"and my position is yours." Remember?' He gestured towards the Doctor and Nyssa. 'Here they are.'

Bor said, 'We all think it's time for a little chat.'

Eirak looked from one to another, all around the room. He was beaten, and he was starting to perceive it.

The Doctor said, 'Before you start, perhaps one of you could show us the way back to the liner. There's still a lot to be done.'

The workload that the Doctor had in mind included effective decontamination of both the TARDIS and its occupants, and repair of the damage that had projected them into this situation in the first place. When this had been carried out, the Doctor intended to leave the decontamination gear for the Vanir to use. There was no way that he could reverse the radiation damage that they'd already suffered, but at least he could slow its effects.

Olvir and Kari had already made their own plans. They were going to take the next 'clean boat' out and start a search for the Chief.

'Nobody ditches us and gets away with it,' Kari said.

There was one other issue to be resolved. But the Doctor knew that it wasn't in his hands.

He and Nyssa were taken to the docking platform by Valgard. The liner's door was still sealed, but Valgard took a complex metal shape from under his cloak and placed it on the outer skin alongside the air-seal.

'It'll be a relief to see the TARDIS again,' the Doctor said.

'And Tegan,' Nyssa added. A flicker of doubt showed in the Doctor's eyes. Through all of the trouble they'd experienced since their arrival, he'd at least been able to console himself with the thought that two of his companions were safely outside the danger area. But why couldn't he feel confident?

The door raised itself automatically, and Tegan stood before them.

She looked a mess. Her clothes were torn and she was smeared with dirt and grease from head to foot. There were streaks across her forehead where she'd tried to wipe sweat away with an oily hand.

The Doctor's worst fears had been realised. 'What are you doing?' he said, and he was obviously annoyed.

'I was trying to reach you,' Tegan said, scrambling to get her ideas together. One moment she'd been looking for a way of opening an impossible door, the next moment it had opened. 'Turlough went back to the TARDIS on his own.'

'I told you not to follow me.'

'Doctor,' Nyssa urged, trying to be conciliatory, 'Say you're pleased to see her.'

155

'I *am* pleased to see her,' the Doctor snapped, sounding quite the opposite. 'But she shouldn't have tried to follow us.'

'You don't understand,' Tegan began, but the Doctor wasn't prepared to listen.

'We'll talk about it later,' he said, and then he and Valgard went through into the liner.

Tegan looked after them, dismayed. 'Why is it always the same?' she said.

'There's a lot to do,' Nyssa said.

'There's always a lot to do.'

Nyssa took her arm. 'Tegan,' she began delicately, 'I have to tell you something.'

Valgard and the Doctor were already some way ahead. Tegan looked after them for a moment. She hadn't yet told the Doctor about the complex sequence of events that governed the appearance and disappearance of the door to the TARDIS. Well, let him find out for himself, since he didn't want to hear what she had to say. Turlough had already done the work of solving the puzzle, and when the maintenance drones had finished their repairs on the automated control centre then the launch sequence would resume and the doorway would return. She turned to Nyssa.

The Doctor, meanwhile, was discussing strategy with Valgard. 'You need publicity,' he was saying. 'Get rid of the secrecy that surrounds this place, and Terminus Incorporated won't be able to do anything against you. Forget the shame and the mystery, and emphasize the treatment.'

'There isn't any treatment without the Garm,' Valgard pointed out. 'You've seen to that.'

'I took away the compulsion, that's all. I'm sure

156

you'll have no problem if you invite him to co-operate.'

'Co-operate?' Valgard said with some incredulity. 'The Garm? You're joking. The Garm's just a dumb beast.'

'Then I think you've got a surprise coming,' the Doctor said.

They were about to climb the stairs between decks, but a loud protest from behind made them stop. The Doctor looked back and saw Tegan, shocked and worried, pulling Nyssa forward.

'Doctor,' Tegan was saying, 'Doctor, talk to her!'

Nyssa was looking at the ground, and she seemed a little embarrassed at being made the sudden focus of attention in this way. The Doctor said, 'What is it?'

Nyssa looked up at him. 'I'm not coming with you,' she said.

And, deep inside, he'd known it. He'd known from the moment he'd seen her again, eyes blazing with righteous fury at the poor excuse for a caring process that she'd been put through. Lives were changed by such experiences, and there was no going back.

'There's the Hydromel to be synthesised, and I can do it,' she added. 'That's what I was trained for. I don't regret one moment of the time that I've spent on the TARDIS and I'll miss you both, but I'm needed here and I'm not going to walk away.'

'Please, Nyssa,' Tegan said tearfully, but Nyssa wasn't to be shaken.

'My mind's made up,' she said. 'Let's not fall out over it.'

The Doctor said, gently, 'I suppose you understand the commitment you'll be taking on.'

Nyssa nodded. 'Yes.'

'And that life here's going to be hard. Not to mention dangerous for a while.'

'And interesting, and fulfilling ...'

'All right,' the Doctor said, holding up his hand and smiling. He'd got the message. Nyssa was fully aware of what she was taking on, and she was determined. With some pressure he might just be able to dissuade her, but he doubted it. And it would be something they'd both regret, for ever.

For Tegan, the enormity of the moment obscured all long-term considerations. 'She'll die here,' she said, almost wailing.

'Not easily, Tegan,' Nyssa told her. 'We're both alike. Indestructible.'

And then they hung onto each other tightly for a few moments. The Doctor watched. It had happened before and it would happen again, and it seemed that the loss of every member of his ever-changing team took a little piece of him away with them. They were spread through time and through space, all of them reshaped and given new insights through their travels.

Their loss wasn't too bad a price to pay ... not when they gave him a kind of immortality.

He turned to Valgard. As he'd said, there was still a lot to be done.

Turlough groaned as he came around. Every bone in his body seemed to have been shaken and twisted. Even the backs of his eyes hurt. He wanted nothing more than to lie on the hard floor of the console room, savouring the relief of not moving.

But the Black Guardian had other plans.

'*Boy*?' he was whispering. '*Wake up, boy.*'

Turlough tried to open his eyes, to lift his head. He made it on the second attempt, and was immediately sorry.

'*The Doctor is returning.*'

He struggled to get the console room into focus. He could remember a blinding light, and the pain that had come with it. The blackness that had followed had been bliss, but it hadn't lasted.

The contact cube was on the floor about a metre away. It was blackened and charred, useless-looking. Turlough said, 'What did you do to me?'

'*You will recover.*'

But if the cube was ruined, how ... Turlough still couldn't think straight. 'I can't do it,' he said. 'Kill the Doctor yourself, I don't care. I just can't go on.'

Darkness filled his vision from side to side, and Turlough looked up in awe as his controller stood over him, the very spirit of evil set walking. The Black Guardian's breath sent a chill across his skin.

'*This is your last chance. I will not say that again. You will kill the Doctor!*'

Turlough had failed once. It seemed he wasn't to be allowed to fail twice.

FANTASTIC
DOCTOR WHO
POSTER OFFER!

Pin up a magnificent full colour poster of Peter Davison as the Doctor, surrounded by a galaxy of Target novelisations – Free!

THIS OFFER EXCLUSIVE TO DOCTOR WHO READERS

Just send £2.50 to cover postage and packing

TO:
Publicity Department
W. H. Allen & Co. Ltd
44 Hill Street
London W1X 8LB

We will send you a **FREE FULL COLOUR POSTER** on receipt of your order.
Please allow **28 days** for delivery.

Please send me a WORLD OF DOCTOR WHO poster.

I enclose £2.50 to cover postage and packing.

Name _____

Address_____

_____

_____

_____

_____

_____